# Sunshine. Sandalwood.
# Pure unadulterated man

Back at The White Elephant, Maggie groaned aloud and rested her head in her hands. In her wildest dreams she would never have imagined herself in such a compromising position on the floor of the Bronze Penguin in full view of half the restaurant.

There was nothing even remotely romantic about what had passed between her and John Adams Tyler. Why, then, was she finding it so impossible to forget the way his body had felt beneath hers?

The jut of his hipbones against the yielding flesh of her inner thighs. The scrape of beard against her cheek as she checked his breathing. The powerful muscles hidden beneath the sober Brooks Brothers shirt.

"Sex," she said.

You could run away from your memories.

You could run away from your fantasies.

But there was no escaping biology. It was there waiting to get you when you least expected it.

# ABOUT THE AUTHOR

Barbara Bretton is no stranger to adventure. She claims that since her move to New Jersey a couple of years ago, her life has *not* been dull. Her husband and two parrots could attest to that. Here, in *Honeymoon Hotel*, Barbara returns to the PAX organization she created in #193 *Playing for Time*, taking us all on another adventure.

## Books by Barbara Bretton

HARLEQUIN AMERICAN ROMANCE
3–LOVE CHANGES
49–THE SWEETEST OF DEBTS
91–NO SAFE PLACE
138–THE EDGE OF FOREVER
161–PROMISES IN THE NIGHT
175–SHOOTING STAR
193–PLAYING FOR TIME
211–SECOND HARMONY
230–NOBODY'S BABY

HARLEQUIN INTRIGUE
18–STARFIRE

# Honeymoon Hotel
## Barbara Bretton

# Harlequin Books

TORONTO • NEW YORK • LONDON
AMSTERDAM • PARIS • SYDNEY • HAMBURG
STOCKHOLM • ATHENS • TOKYO • MILAN

For Robin and Bob and the Joyce Kilmer Rest Stop
on that dark and stormy night and
For Deby, who understands that truth is sometimes
stranger than.

Published June 1988

First printing April 1988

ISBN 0-373-16251-0

# Chapter One

"Mirrored ceilings are a necessary evil," said Alistair Chambers as he reached for his brandy. "Utterly unavoidable."

"Hah!" Holland Masters stabbed the innocent strawberry tart on her plate with a silver fork. "Only if you're twenty-two and perfect. Who wants to see cellulite and spider veins in 3-D?"

The beautiful redhead shivered delicately and, across the table, Maggie Douglass chuckled into her chocolate mousse.

For the past hour Maggie had been refereeing a lively discussion on the relative merits of interior design à la the Pocono Mountains.

Her debonair Uncle Alistair had come down squarely on the side of water beds and champagne-glass whirlpools for two, while the bohemian Ms. Masters had surprised both of them by casting her vote for the more conservative pleasures to be found in candlelight and roaring fires.

"You're a snob," said Alistair to his ladylove.

"And you're an unrepentant rake." Holland, an actress, launched into a detailed and dramatic explanation of his more libertine tendencies that on another day might have tickled Maggie's sense of the absurd.

But not today.

What was the matter with those two anyway? Who needed bubble baths and soft music to woo a willing partner?

Any fool knew that when it came to seduction, the name of the game was chocolate.

Especially the Bronze Penguin's chocolate mousse.

There wasn't a man alive who could compete.

At least that's what Maggie Douglass thought until the moment she saw him stride into the restaurant.

She stopped dead, her third spoonful halfway to her lips, and stared as the handsome stranger followed Claude, the imperious maître d', to the VIP table near the French doors—the same table the surly Claude had patently refused her not one hour ago.

There weren't many things on earth that could take her mind away from chocolate mousse with freshly whipped cream, but a gorgeous man in a charcoal-gray suit was definitely one of them.

It wasn't often you saw men in Savile Row suits in East Point, Pennsylvania—not even at the venerable Bronze Penguin, the Poconos' answer to Lutece.

To see two Savile Row suits in the same place on the same day—well, that was definitely worth a second look.

Not that Maggie wouldn't have given him a second look anyway. Men like that belonged to her other life, to dinners at Maxim's and summers in Monte Carlo.

East Point was nestled snugly in the midst of the Pocono Mountains, and most men as gorgeous as this one usually came with a brand-new blushing bride in tow. To see a tall, handsome stranger who was obviously alone was nothing short of extraordinary.

No wonder Claude was tumbling over his wing tips with excitement.

"My favorite table," Maggie mumbled, covering up her own ardent interest with righteous indignation. "And to a perfect stranger, no less!"

Holland halted her discourse on heart-shaped bathtubs long enough to follow Maggie's gaze. "Definitely perfect," she drawled in the same throaty voice enjoyed by millions, five days a week on *Destiny*, the nation's number one soap. "He gives new meaning to the cliché, tall, dark and handsome."

Alistair, the owner of the other Savile Row suit on display that Wednesday afternoon in August, cleared his throat and motioned for brandy all around. "I'll concede two of your three observations, but one can scarcely tell if the gentleman in question is tall when he's seated."

"He's tall," Maggie said, looking away as the stranger met her eyes. He had towered over Claude and, even seated, he still seemed to dominate the room. She also had the feeling those broad shoulders weren't the result of clever padding by a cunning British tailor, but of coiled muscle beneath.

Her uncle turned to Holland. "How does she know he's tall?"

"Trust her, darling," said Holland. "There are some things a woman just knows."

Maggie glanced back in time to see Claude present the man a menu with a flourish reserved for visiting royalty.

"I live in this town," Maggie grumbled, attacking her defenseless mousse again. "Shouldn't that count for something?"

"To the rich belong the spoils," said Alistair. "The way to Claude's heart is through his wallet. Obviously your perfect man is not above bribery."

"That's not bribery," Maggie retorted. "That's blackmail."

As the owner of The White Elephant, the least well-known honeymoon resort in the Poconos, Maggie Douglass was hard-pressed to pay for this lunch. She certainly wasn't in any position to add an arrogant maître d' to her payroll.

Leave that to the new owner of Hideaway Haven with its patented Love Cottages that came complete with flocked velvet wallpaper and hot- and cold-running Jacuzzis. The way rumor said the new owner was raking in the bucks, he could afford Claude's blackmail money.

"Stop mumbling like a country girl," Holland said, sipping her brandy. "You've been here in the backwoods too long, Maggie. In Manhattan maître d's rule the world."

"This isn't Manhattan."

"Really?" Holland murmured, her green eyes twinkling. "I hadn't noticed."

Maggie laughed despite herself. Let Claude enjoy his power trip all he wanted. She wouldn't trade her lunch companions for the best table in the house.

Not even if that gorgeous stranger came with it.

THE SECOND the lanky maître d' with the Charles de Gaulle profile oiled his way over to him, John Adams Tyler knew he should have gone to McDonald's instead.

But McDonald's wasn't safe, any more than Burger King or Sizzler or any of the other middle-class bastions of fast food were safe. If he wanted to avoid the men who were dogging his steps, he would just have to put up with this kind of pretentious garbage.

He glanced around the place and stifled a groan as somewhere in the vastness, a champagne cork popped.

He hated fancy restaurants. He hated French food. And, more than anything, he hated maître d's.

"Tyler," he said as the man scanned his reservation book. "Table for one."

Claude took a long look at John, obviously checking for signs of wealth. His gaze slid over the expensive silk suit and the de rigueur gold watch, then stuttered over the longer-than-average hair that tickled John's collar.

That stutter was quickly smoothed over when John pressed a twenty-dollar bill into Claude's eager palm.

"Ah, yes!" The bill disappeared into the pocket of Claude's trousers. "Your name is indeed on the list." He closed the book and gave John a courtly, if obsequious, bow. "This way, sir."

Social snobbery in the Poconos, where Love Tubs and Magic Fingers were the ultimate status symbols?

Amazing.

Yet the most amazing thing of all was that John Adams Tyler, aka The Animal, had been quick enough to play by the same rules he'd poked fun at a million years ago.

Maybe that's why he'd ducked out of the last meeting and hidden away here at the Bronze Penguin where none of the people who mattered would ever look.

He needed time to think. They'd been dogging his steps for months now, trying to pull him back into a past he wanted to forget.

Old memories.

Old debts.

Saying no to them wouldn't be easy.

Claude hovered around like a bird of prey. "Are you certain this table is to your liking, *m'sieur*?"

John unbuttoned his suit jacket. "The table is fine."

"I can bring you our master wine list."

He shook his head. "Not necessary."

"We have a superb Riesling you might consider. I can ask Gerard to bring one up so you can—"

"No Riesling," said John. "No master wine list. No Gerard. Just bring me a Bud and the menu."

Claude scurried off, muttering something about peasant taste, and John laughed for the first time that day.

Peasant taste? He thought about pepperoni pizzas and meatball heros and BLTs, hold the mayo. The Bronze Penguin still had a lot to learn when it came to food.

He'd just spent three of the most boring hours of his life in conference with lawyers and money men who seemed to derive great pleasure out of telling him things couldn't be done.

The family ski resort in New Hampshire couldn't be done.

It grossed three million dollars its first season.

The chain of video stores featuring classic films was doomed to failure.

A front-page story on its success graced last month's *Forbes*.

Now they were trying to convince him that he should sell Hideaway Haven and its patented Love Cottages to the hungry multinational corporation that had been gobbling up much of the Pennsylvania countryside.

He'd probably own the state before it was all over.

He nodded as the affronted Claude deposited a bottle of Bud on the table before him and made a show of pouring it into a heavy crystal mug. A young, dark-haired waiter barely missed bumping into Claude as he hurried through the room with a tray piled high with steamed lobster.

What the hell did the money men know anyway? Facts and figures on cold white paper didn't mean a damn thing. Gut instinct was the only thing worth counting on, and when it came to following his gut instincts, John Adams Tyler was a pro.

Sell Honeymoon Haven?

No way.

He'd keep it and bet that by October he'd have another cool million with which to drive his accountant up the wall in search of tax shelters.

Grinning, John raised his beer mug to his mouth and was about to take a long slug when he saw her watching him.

A woman with a cloud of long coppery-gold waves tumbling over her bare shoulders was looking straight at him. She wore a white cotton sundress that was more style than substance, and it shimmered pale against her tanned skin. Her gaze was level and deliberate, no coy flutter of the eyelashes, no hint of flirtation.

She was seated with a brutally well-tailored man and a gorgeous redhead of a certain age who were holding hands below the table level. They looked familiar. Hadn't he seen them around Hideaway Haven?

If so, where was the younger woman's husband?

And, if there *was* a husband, what the hell was she doing making eye contact with him?

Intrigued, John prepared to lift his glass in salute, when the young waiter bumped against the back of his chair and a splash of beer hit John right between the eyes.

Claude swooped down on him like a heat-seeking missile. "Clumsy fool!" said the maître d'. "Not you, sir, of course." His dream of a hefty tip obviously teetered on the brink. "Please forward your dry-cleaning bill to me, and I'll attend to it personally."

"No damage." John wiped the beer off his face with his napkin. "Just bring me another."

Damn it. Across the room the vision in white was once again engrossed in lively conversation with her table mates, her curiosity in John long forgotten.

The kamikaze waiter made another pass around the room and left another casualty behind.

John leaned back in his chair and opened his menu.

McDonald's next time, no matter how dangerous it was.

MAGGIE COULDN'T REMEMBER the last time she'd enjoyed a lunch the way she was enjoying this one.

Her Aunt Sarah's death had hit Alistair hard. Her uncle had suddenly aged right before her eyes, and Maggie had despaired as he threw himself deeper into his work—and into danger.

His work with PAX, an international antiterrorist organization with a low profile and a high rate of success, had always bordered on obsessive, but since he had shared that obsession with Sarah, who was also a PAX operative, Maggie hadn't been aware of how deep his commitment ran.

After Sarah's death, there was no question.

PAX had sprung to life during World War II as a way of opening communications between the Allies without risking detection by the enemy. Alistair and other faceless couriers moved from battle zone to battle zone, sometimes behind enemy lines, to ensure that vital information made it into the right hands.

Some historians said D-Day would never have happened had it not been for those courageous men and women.

After the war, PAX had continued, and Alistair had continued along with it. The rebuilding of Europe after the war was a delicate business, and the organization, with its multinational members and superior technology, was a necessary factor in restoring a semblance of normalcy to ravaged lands.

It was dangerous work then, and it was dangerous work now, and when his Sarah died it seemed Alistair had made it his business to take on the riskiest assignments available. He had grown older, more jaded with every passing day, and Maggie's heart had ached each time she saw him.

But since meeting Holland Masters two years ago, Alistair Chambers had become a walking advertisement for the fountain of youth. Who would have imagined it was hidden right in the heart of Manhattan?

Alistair would never see sixty again, and Holland was floating delicately in the region of forty-plus, yet every time Maggie was around them, she caught the unmistakable scent of orange blossoms and the thrill of young love in the air.

Not that the scent of orange blossoms wasn't everywhere in the Poconos. For over forty years, couples from every part of the country had been converging on those quiet Pennsylvania mountains to spend a blissful week in one of countless honeymoon hotels scattered throughout the countryside.

Although they seemed better suited for the Swiss Alps, Alistair and Holland obviously liked the all-American Poconos. They'd come up from Manhattan three times in the past three weeks, treating Maggie to wonderful dinners and delightful conversation.

Maggie couldn't help but wonder if there was some deeper reason for this sudden interest in honeymoon hotels but, knowing her uncle as she did, she'd find out soon enough.

As it was, Maggie was savoring the opportunity to enjoy the very romantic courtship of her favorite uncle and his ladylove who, at the moment, seemed to have an unholy fixation with mirrors and lights.

"Okay," Maggie said, gesturing with her dessert spoon. "Why all this talk about mirrors on the ceiling? The White Elephant doesn't have mirrors on the ceiling. The only way you could—" She stopped at the guilty expression on her usually unflappable uncle's face. "You didn't!"

"I'm afraid we did," said Alistair.

"You went over to the competition?"

"It seemed a marvelous idea at the time." He glanced at Holland for support. "How better to understand what battles you've yet to face? A little discreet investigating seemed apropos."

"I fought the good fight," said Holland. "I brought up family loyalty, moral rectitude and possible public humiliation." She shrugged eloquently. "Nothing worked."

Maggie polished off her last spoonful of chocolate mousse and took a quick, longing peek at Holland's strawberry tart. "My own flesh and blood goes over to the enemy camp."

"Don't you want to know what the competition is doing, dear girl? Holland and I can give you an on-the-spot description of everything that goes on at the Love Cottages."

Holland blanched visibly. "Not everything."

"We can supply you with demographics on the clientele."

"We didn't see any of the clientele all weekend."

Alistair winked at Maggie. "We can supply pictures and—"

"Oh, no, we can't," Holland broke in. "Not unless I retouch a few negatives."

"Go ahead," said Alistair, puffing on a Gauloise. "Ask me anything about the Love Cottages."

Maggie, who was consumed with curiosity, feigned indifference. "Purple shag rugs and lava lights aren't my idea of class. I have loftier aims for The White Elephant."

Alistair pierced her with a look. "Some people find purple shag rugs very romantic."

"I'm not some people."

"Do you find anything romantic these days, Maggie?"

She faked a swoon at the sight of the dessert cart rolling by their table. "Be careful, Holland," she said. "Your strawberry tart is in peril."

"Don't change the subject," said her uncle. "I'm concerned. Certainly there must be some eligible men here in honeymoon heaven."

Maggie groaned. "I get enough of the romance-is-where-you-find-it routine from the Douglass clan."

"And well you should. You're much too young and beautiful to bury yourself in that monstrosity you call an inn. When was the last time you were out on a date?"

"Last month," Maggie shot back to Holland's applause. "Craig Watson. Three hours trapped in a bowling alley with a man whose idea of a good time is a seventen split." In the four years since her husband, Rick's, death, Maggie was certain she'd suffered through more blind dates than Helen Keller.

"So Mr. Watson was an unmitigated boor," said Alistair. "Surely you've had some good dates recently."

"That *was* a good date." She turned to Holland. "Tell him there's nothing wrong with being single, please!"

"Not I," said Holland with a short laugh. "That's a definite conflict of interests."

In retaliation Maggie swiped a piece of Holland's unguarded strawberry tart. "I like where I live. I like how I live. I like with whom I live." No one dared dangle a preposition around Alistair Chambers.

"You live with a foul-tempered parrot." Alistair brushed off bread crumbs scattered by a birdbrained waiter. "Yours is hardly the usual housemate."

She thought of The White Elephant with its spires and turrets and occasional newlyweds. "Mine is hardly the usual house."

"You're a difficult woman, Magdalena," said Alistair. "I'm only thinking of your happiness."

Maggie groaned. "Alistair, so help me, if you say one more word about my social life, I'm leaving you with the bill."

"Listen to her, darling," said Holland with a grin. "We ordered champagne and caviar."

Maggie couldn't help laughing, but a sharp edge of truth poked through. "Besides," she said, "you're asking for the impossible. Single men in the Poconos are rare as truffles."

Holland gestured toward the man across the room. "How about that gorgeous specimen? He's been watching you ever since he sat down."

So she hadn't imagined his interest.

Maggie glanced in his direction. "He's probably a bubble bath salesman with a wife and eight kids waiting for him at home."

"So you *did* notice him!" Holland patted Alistair's forearm. "See? There's hope for her yet."

"This has to be the most ridiculous conversation I've ever had." Which was saying a great deal, since water beds and mirrored ceilings had been the featured topics earlier in the luncheon. "Just because I refuse to paper the guest rooms with scenes from the Kama Sutra doesn't mean I'm ready for a rocking chair yet."

"Then prove it, darling," said Holland. "Go over there and strike up a conversation with your admirer."

Maggie took a long look at him as he demolished a piece of Chicken Kiev. God, he was enthusiastic.

"Forget it," she said. "He's not my type."

Holland's coffee cup clattered against its saucer. "Not your type! You have something against tall, dark and handsome hunks?"

"Yes," Maggie replied cheerfully. "They're usually stupid."

Alistair cleared his throat. "I, for one, am feeling inordinately uncomfortable at this moment."

"So am I," said Maggie. "I suggest we leave the subject of my social life alone."

Alistair recovered his composure in record time. "I have but a few more things to say on that subject, and then we can—"

"Remember what I said before," Maggie warned, with a wicked gleam in her eye.

"—move on to other items. You're too young to resign yourself to a—"

"Alistair! I'm warning you...."

"—life of loneliness and—"

Maggie pushed back her chair and stood up. "Thank you," she said, flashing a triumphant smile. "Lunch is on you."

*DAMN IT TO HELL!*

The woman in the white dress was leaving.

Not ten feet away from him she was making her way through the crowded dining room and heading straight for the door.

For the last thirty minutes he'd toyed with the idea of sending her a bottle of Moët, or a note inviting her out to dinner. He'd even considered sauntering over to her table and introducing himself.

But, in the end, he did none of these.

He sat there drinking Bud under Claude's disapproving eye, and wondering why some things got harder to do as you got older.

It didn't seem fair.

In a logical world, age and experience would make this sort of thing easier.

Hell.

Ten years ago he wouldn't have hesitated.

Ten years ago he would have walked right up to her and stated his intentions, and he wouldn't have given her the chance to say no.

But he was thirty-five now and as far removed from The Animal as Santa Claus was from Satan. He'd learned the hard way that you don't always get what you want—and that what you get isn't always what you need.

He cut into his chicken and took a long hard look at the fancy butter and herbs running all over his plate.

What in hell was he doing eating Chicken Kiev anyway?

He was getting soft, that's what it was.

Old and soft.

The hard edge that saw him through the low spots had vanished along with money problems and touring and the rush of excitement he'd felt each time he took the stage.

The kamikaze waiter raced past with a tray of sizzling steaks, and he just missed bumping into the woman in white who was stopped near the door, chatting with a tall skinny guy who'd interviewed John for the *Pocono Bugle*.

John cut another piece of chicken and watched her. The reporter said something, and she threw her head back and laughed, a low, slightly husky sound that was everything he'd imagined her laugh would be.

What the hell was he waiting for anyway?

In another second she'd turn and walk out of the restaurant and out of his life.

*Say something, you idiot! Don't let her get away!*

He pushed away from the table before he'd even finished chewing his last piece of Chicken Kiev.

He didn't see the doomsday waiter racing back toward the kitchen until it was too late.

"I'm s-sorry, sir," the waiter stammered. "I didn't see you—sir?" The waiter's eyes bugged out as he stared at John. "Sir? Are you all right?"

But John wasn't all right.

"Sir? Sir! Say something, sir!"

*I can't say anything, you jerk! I can't even breathe!*

What a way to go: choked to death by a piece of Chicken Kiev at the Bronze Penguin in East Point, Pennsylvania.

If asphyxiation didn't kill him, he was damned sure embarrassment would.

It was going to make one hell of an obituary.

He dropped to his knees as everything around him swirled white, then red, then finally faded to black.

Too bad he wouldn't be around to enjoy it.

# Chapter Two

This wasn't exactly the grand exit Maggie had planned when she left Alistair and Holland with the bill. She'd wanted to at least make it out to the parking lot before the two of them did.

As it was, she didn't even make it to the door before Frank Kraemer from the *Pocono Bugle* flagged her down and managed to involved her in a five-way discussion on the hotel owners' meeting coming up in two weeks.

"We want to tie it in with the magazine Arnie Sandler is putting together," Frank said as she refused his third offer to have a quick drink with them. "What would you say about sitting down for an in-depth interview with me next week?"

"Terrific," she said as she watched Alistair dig into his pocket for his platinum American Express card. "Call me at the office, and I'll see how my schedule is."

Everyone at the table laughed. Maggie's lack of visitors at The White Elephant was a running joke.

She turned to make her escape when, from across the restaurant, a woman's scream bounced off the high-beamed ceiling and filled the room. Claude, minus his legendary sophistication, was staring, horrified, as a knot of people gathered near the French doors.

"Call 911!" the imperious maître d' shouted, his voice shrill. "We have a heart attack in progress!"

The restaurant fell silent.

No hysteria.

No commotion.

Nobody racing to the phones to get help.

Suddenly it all came back to her.

"Make the call from your cellular phone," she called to Alistair. "Have them send an ambulance."

"You remember CPR?"

Memories of Rick washed over her, and she waited a moment while the pain flared, then flickered away. "I remember."

Her uncle hurried from the restaurant with Holland close behind.

Maggie made her way toward the crowd of people near the French doors. What was the matter with everybody?

Some poor old man or woman was going into cardiac seizure, and these fools were watching as if it were the cliff-hanger episode on *Dallas*.

Lying on the floor in front of the best table in the Bronze Penguin was the magnificent man in the dark suit who'd been the object of her lunchtime fantasies.

His silk tie had been loosened, and one end drifted across his handsome face. His shirt had been ripped open, exposing a tanned chest that was everything she'd imagined it would be.

And only the most incredible female swine would notice any of those things with a man dying at her feet.

"He just keeled over," said a woman in a green cotton shirtwaist. She pointed toward the clumsy waiter who'd made much of lunch an adventure. "Right after that clumsy fool bumped into his chair."

"Hey, wait a minute!" The clumsy-fool waiter stumbled into the center of the crowd. "Don't go blaming a heart attack on me! All I did was bump into him with a tray of baked potato shells. You can't go laying this one on me!"

"Nobody said it was your fault," the woman shot back. "I'm just relating the facts."

"The facts!" Claude broke in. "I'll give you the facts. What we have here is—"

"Shut up!" Maggie's words split the air the way the woman's scream had a few moments ago. "I don't give a damn who did what to whom. Does he have a pulse?"

Claude nodded.

Maggie knelt down next to the man. He seemed to be unconscious. His face was pale and suspiciously blue tinged. One of his large hands rested near his throat.

She ripped open his shirt the rest of the way, and placed her ear against his mouth.

Nothing.

Sweat broke out on the back of her neck and she— thank God! A pulse still hammered in his carotid artery.

Wait a minute. Something didn't make sense. The pulse was too strong for a heart attack, and the way his hand seemed to clutch his throat—

She zeroed in on Claude. "Quick! Tell me exactly what happened." She pulled off the man's tie and began to position his head for resuscitation.

"Martin bumped into him. The man looked around then suddenly jumped up." The upended chair near the table was testament to just how quickly the man had jumped.

"Did he clutch his chest or grab his shoulder?"

Claude shook his head. "He didn't do anything. He just stood up, then fell over."

Martin, the clumsy waiter, stepped forward, his face as pale as the man on the floor. "He did do something," he said, looking at Maggie. "He grabbed his neck like this."

"This isn't a heart attack," Maggie said, praying her intuition was right. "He's choking to death."

"He's unconscious." Claude stepped back as if he wanted to disappear into the throng gathered around them. "There's nothing you can do. Wait for the emergency crew to get here."

"He'll be dead by then." Maggie thanked God for full skirts as she hiked her hem up over her thighs and straddled the man's hips. Placing her hands one atop the other, she positioned the heel of the bottom hand just above his navel and, whispering a silent prayer, she hoped Dr. Heimlich and his famous maneuver would come to the rescue just one more time.

HE WAS DEAD.

That had to be it.

He was dead, and this was heaven, or at least one of the stops along the way to the pearly gates.

He'd been drifting someplace far away, his mind a whirl of color and sound, when suddenly he found himself staring at a red-haired angel who looked a hell of a lot like the woman he'd been admiring at the Bronze Penguin just before he died.

But wait a minute!

He wasn't an expert on theology, and he had no idea how many angels could dance on the head of a pin, but he was pretty damned sure no self-respecting angel would be caught in this position.

"Chicken Kiev." Her voice was definitely heaven-sent.

They said hearing was the last to go. Maybe she would be his last glimpse of the mortal world.

He blinked once.

Twice.

The scent of Shalimar teased his nostrils. The wildly exotic creature with the long coppery-blond hair was still there, with one leg pressed against each of his thighs.

He doubted if dead men were allowed to enjoy pleasures like this one.

"What?" His voice sounded as rough and raw as his throat felt.

"Chicken Kiev," she repeated, smiling down at him. Her eyes were a pure cornflower blue. "It's a killer."

Was he supposed to know what she was talking about? "I don't understand. What—" He stopped as it all came back to him in humiliating detail.

She laughed, still astride him, and that incredible mane of hair danced around her shoulders. "Remember now?"

"I was choking to death." What an amazing statement!

"Quite effectively, I might add," she said, beginning to button his shirt. "You gave everyone a scare."

He grabbed her wrists, and she met his eyes. "You saved my life?"

She shrugged, her wrists still captured in his grasp. "It was a dirty job, but someone had to do it."

Some nervous laughter behind him made John realize they had an audience.

"Get serious," he snapped, embarrassment getting the better of him. His body had recovered quicker than his brain and was taking full advantage of the situation. "You saved my life, right?"

She yanked her hands away from him and tossed his tie in his direction. It landed on his head.

"Yes," she said, "but don't let it go to your head."

"I can't believe it."

"You're breathing, aren't you?" She sounded as if she was having second thoughts on the matter. "That should be proof enough."

"How did you know what to do?"

She snapped her fingers. "Nothing any ex-Girl Scout couldn't do."

The un-Girl Scout-like position she was in must have suddenly dawned on her because she scrambled to her feet, but not before he had a glimpse of her silky white slip and her even silkier tanned legs.

In fact, with her standing over him, his vantage point on the floor of the Bronze Penguin wasn't half-bad.

Unfortunately she was as smart as she was beautiful, and she extended her hand to him.

"Come on," she said, a smile dancing around the corners of her mouth. "You're enjoying this too much."

He grasped her hand and hoisted himself to his feet. She'd seemed like an Amazon warrior when he awoke and saw her looming over him—all beautiful, womanly concern. Face-to-face she was even more overwhelming.

"Doesn't a dying man have any rights?" he asked as the crowd dispersed now that the excitement was over.

She withdrew her hand from his once again. "You're not a dying man."

"I'd be a dead man if you hadn't jumped on me."

She blushed beneath her tan. Incredible. He hadn't seen a woman blush since the summer of 1968.

"I didn't jump on you," she said, smoothing down her skirts. "I performed a lifesaving maneuver."

"So you admit you saved my life."

"I admit nothing. I did what needed to be done."

"You're a hero," he said, ignoring Frank Kraemer from the *Pocono Bugle* as the man tried to jockey into picture-taking position. "If you hadn't climbed on top of me, they'd be writing my obituary right now."

"If you don't stop saying things like that, they *will* be writing your obituary."

"I love it," said Frank. "She saves the life of her number-one competitor. This is front-page copy."

They both wheeled and faced him. "What?" they asked in unison.

"You two know each other, don't you?"

Once again, in unison, they shook their heads.

Frank seemed to be getting an unholy kick out of the situation. "John," he said, "I'd like you to meet Maggie Douglass, owner of The White Elephant at the foot of Mount Snow."

"The White Elephant? You don't mean that old—"

"Watch it!" Maggie snapped. "That old place happens to mean a lot to me."

"I know," said John, shaking her hand under Frank's gleeful eye. "I tried to buy it from you last year."

"Oh, no," she groaned. "Don't tell me you're—"

"John Adams Tyler."

"Not the same Tyler who owns Hideaway Haven and those damned Love Cottages."

"One and the same."

"I can't believe you two haven't met before this," said Frank as he snapped a picture of them shaking hands. "I thought all you owners knew one another."

"So did I," said Maggie, fixing him with her baby-blue stare. "It seems Mr. Tyler doesn't like to bother with the rest of us. After all, I've never seen you at any of our meetings."

"An oversight that I've already taken steps to correct," John said. "I joined the hotel owners' association and intend to be present at the next meeting."

"To promote the proliferation of heart-shaped bathtubs, I'm sure."

He laughed at the serious expression on her beautiful face. "This is the Poconos," he said. "Heart-shaped bathtubs are expected of us."

"I refuse to believe there isn't a market for a classier establishment up here."

"We're running at one hundred percent capacity," he said. "How about you?"

Her jaw clenched. "That's an unfair question."

"Eighty percent?"

She said nothing.

"Sixty percent?"

"Forty-eight percent, not that it's any of your business."

"You've dropped since March," he observed. "You're in the red zone."

"Thank you, Mr. Tyler, but I don't recall asking for an analysis of my hotel management skills."

"You just need to update and get in step with the market."

"You just need to mind your own business." She turned to say something to Frank, then suddenly wheeled back to glare at John. "If I'm doing such lousy business, why were you so interested in buying me out?"

"Location." Honesty was one of his best qualities— and the one least appreciated at times like this. "Fifteen prime acres complete with a lake. All those secret passageways beneath your main house fascinate the hell out of me." He grinned. "We could do wonders with it."

"I'm already doing wonders with it." Her lovely eyes narrowed. "How do you know about those secret passageways?"

He'd never seen such towering outrage on someone so angelic looking in his life. A laugh threatened to break through, but he was afraid she'd belt him if he let it out. "Your passageways connect to my barn. You should know that."

"If I know you, you'll end up covering them with purple plush carpeting."

"Lighten up, Ms. Douglass. We're talking honeymoon hotels, not Buckingham Palace."

"I don't care if we're talking bordello-chic, Tyler. Bad taste is bad taste. If you want to live with Jacuzzis shaped like champagne glasses and mirrored ceilings in the bathroom, that's your business."

"We're not talking about decorating the home of your dreams, Ms. Douglass. We're talking fantasy." He couldn't hold back a grin. "You do know about fantasies, don't you?"

"Yes," she said evenly, "and I'm enjoying one right now that has to do with Chicken Kiev."

"Having second thoughts about heroism?"

"You might say that."

"Too late for that," he said, grinning. "I'm hale and hearty."

"Terrific," she mumbled.

It *was* terrific. "You know what this means, don't you, Ms. Douglass? The larger ramifications?"

She shook her head.

"When you saved my life, you joined our fates forever."

"Great," she snapped. "You're in my debt. Just give me a million dollar reward, and we'll call it even."

So she *did* have a sense of humor. He'd begun to wonder.

"It doesn't work that way," he said. "You gave me a second chance. Now I'm your responsibility."

"He's right, Maggie," Frank piped up. "It's an old Chinese tradition."

John reminded himself to take some ads in Frank's paper.

"I'm not old, and I'm not Chinese," said Maggie. "Therefore I'm off the hook."

"You're treating this lightly," John said, fascinated that a woman with such wildly exotic looks could have the prim and proper soul of a Puritan. "You can't believe you can snatch a man from the jaws of death and not bear some responsibility for his life."

She mumbled something about another order of Chicken Kiev, but he decided to ignore it.

"I made you cough up a piece of chicken," she said as they heard sirens wailing in the distance. "If I didn't help you, someone else would have."

"Someone else didn't," he said. "You did."

The sirens came closer.

"Look, just because you haven't mastered solid food yet is no reason for us to become lifelong friends. You thanked me. I acknowledged your thanks. Case closed."

Damn it. It sounded like a fleet of ambulances was racing up the circular drive to the Bronze Penguin.

"Have dinner with me tonight, Maggie Douglass."

She looked down at the overturned table, the upended chair and the mess of chicken and butter on the floor. "Sorry. Dinner with you might be too much of an adventure for me."

"Humor me. I want to thank you properly."

The doors to the restaurant crashed open, and a squad of emergency technicians with CPR on their minds flooded the restaurant.

"A million dollars," said Maggie with a heart-crunching smile as two burly technicians started slapping electrodes on his exposed chest. "Send it in care of The White Elephant."

She was gone before he had a chance to tell the technicians that the change in his heartbeat didn't have a damned thing to do with his health.

It had to do with the woman he intended to marry.

# Chapter Three

*Sunshine.*

*Sandalwood.*

*Pure unadulterated man.*

Maggie groaned out loud and rested her head in her hands.

For the past hour she'd been sitting at her computer, trying to make some sense out of her inventory records and coming up empty.

Well, not exactly empty.

Where she was supposed to enter the number of units, she'd keyed in *6'3"*.

When it asked for the total meals projected for the following month, she'd typed in *molten gold*, the color of his eyes.

And where she was supposed to be listing her current assets, she found herself listing the assets of one John Adams Tyler.

Thank God, Alistair and Holland had gone off to do some antiquing.

The last thing Maggie needed was for anyone else to be a witness to this crazy teenybopper reaction she was having to the owner of the tacky, tasteless and *extremely* popular Hideaway Haven and its Love Cottages.

"Sex," she said to Groucho, the big green parrot sitting atop her computer. That's all it was, of course. A simple physical response to being that close to a member of the opposite sex.

Groucho said nothing, he simply lowered his head to have his feathers scratched.

"Just like a man," she mumbled. Always thinking about physical satisfaction.

Of course, she was a fine one to talk. All afternoon she'd been thinking of nothing else but. If she was a decent sort of woman, she'd be dusting off her Girl Scout badges and congratulating herself on saving a hapless man's life.

Instead she found herself wondering how that hapless man would look with that white shirt of his unbuttoned the rest of the way.

In her wildest dreams she would never have imagined herself in such a compromising position on the floor of the Bronze Penguin in full view of half the hotel owners in East Point—and the *Pocono Bugle*'s star reporter, to boot.

There was nothing even remotely romantic about what had passed between her and John Adams Tyler; in fact, from the moment he had resumed breathing, they'd sparred with each other like two heavyweight contenders going for the title.

Why then was she finding it so impossible to forget the way his body had felt beneath hers?

The jut of hipbones against the yielding flesh of her inner thighs. The scrape of beard against her cheek as she checked his breathing. The powerful muscles hidden beneath that sober Brooks Brothers shirt.

He wasn't even her type with that expensive suit and tailored haircut. She liked men who looked windblown.

Men who looked as if they understood how to change snow tires and repair roofs.

Why, he probably stood in front of the gold-veined mirror in one of his Versailles-gone-amok bathrooms at Hideaway Haven fluffing his hair with a precious little blow-dryer.

"Sex," she said again. Definitely sex.

You could run away from your memories; you could run away from your fantasies. But there was no escaping biology.

It was there waiting to get you when you least expected it. A woman in her thirties was a force to be reckoned with.

Of course her body went crazy this afternoon. Why wouldn't it? The last time she'd been that close to a man, that man had been her husband, and she'd known every angle and muscle of his body as intimately as she knew her own.

Groucho fluttered his wings at Maggie. "Sex!" he squawked, bobbing his head.

She tossed a peanut at him, and he caught it neatly in his beak. "Mind your own business," she said, laughing, "or I'm going to get a cat."

Or a turtle or a rabbit. Something that wouldn't blurt out her secrets at the drop of a peanut.

She shut off the computer and headed upstairs to take a shower.

A cold one.

HIDEAWAY HAVEN, with its patented Love Cottages, was situated atop Mount Ryan. It was snuggled in between two natural lakes and a view of the countryside so beautiful it could be declared a natural wonder.

Not that John noticed any of it that afternoon as he drove back from the Bronze Penguin.

He didn't notice the purple-blue gentian blazing in the late summer sun or the fading bluets or the Dutchman's-breeches with their ridiculous white flowers that looked like knickers on a clothesline.

Pine trees raced towering oaks for a piece of the clear Pennsylvania sky that could have been the skyline of beautiful downtown Burbank for all John saw.

It took all his concentration to keep his mind on his driving because his imagination was running riot. All he could think of was the way Maggie Douglass had felt as she straddled his body. With every breath he took, he smelled the sweet scent of her skin, heard her husky voice murmuring the romantic words "Chicken Kiev" in his ear.

But, of course, none of this was any surprise to John.

John Adams Tyler was a dyed-in-the-wool romantic, one of a long line of romantics that had begun with his ancestor, John Adams, who had loved Abigail for all time.

The men in his family were famous for falling victim to love at first sight, and although a few of them had gone astray, most of the Adams/Tyler men had been lucky enough to form little dynasties of their own.

All of them, that is, except John.

While his brothers had managed to carry on the tradition of happily-ever-after, John resolutely remained single.

He liked women, really liked them. He respected their intelligence, enjoyed their wit, savored their beauty. Twice he'd come close to marriage, but each time, the woman in question had been smarter than he and recognized his fatal flaw.

John Adams Tyler wanted it all.

He wanted passion and romance. He wanted a best friend and a lover and a companion to travel through life with.

He wanted what Adams after Adams after Adams had sought throughout the years: He wanted a wife.

Hell, he wanted to be a husband.

Of course, it had taken him a while to realize it.

His family had teased him and worried over him and tried to fix him up with every beautiful single woman they could find whose IQ was larger than her bra size. He'd done a fair amount of searching on his own, and while he'd formed friendships with a number of the ladies, he'd never found the one he could imagine growing old beside.

Until today.

Who would have thought he'd meet the woman of his dreams while he was lying on the floor of the Bronze Penguin?

Just last weekend his terminal bachelor status had been the topic of heated debate. He and his brothers had thrown a golden wedding anniversary party for their parents. It had all been there, right in front of him, three generations of dreams and hopes and glory, from the remarkable Grandma Rose right down to the newborn Michael.

For the first time in his life, he'd wondered if he'd made a mistake. Maybe he'd waited too long, been too optimistic, let his intrepid belief in romantic destiny turn him into a ninety-seven-year-old fool whose tombstone would read STILL LOOKING.

And it had all changed today in the blink of an eye.

He eased his Jaguar past honeymooners on horseback, honeymooners on bicycles, honeymooners on their—well, maybe some things were better left to the imagination. He beeped his horn in salute as two new-lyweds dived for cover behind a welcoming pine tree.

There wasn't anywhere you could look on that entire sprawling piece of Pennsylvania prime property that you didn't see men and women in love. It was as inescapable as the sunrise each morning, the star rise each night.

Where better to conduct a courtship than right there in the middle of all this bucolic, romantic splendor?

He couldn't miss.

But first he had to get her attention.

"I DON'T THINK Maggie's happy," Holland said, three antique shops after the Bronze Penguin lunch. "Did you notice how quiet she was this afternoon?"

"Of course she was quiet," said Alistair as they backed out of the parking lot of The Ink-Stained Wretch, a used bookstore at the edge of town. "You didn't give her a chance to speak, Holland."

Leave it to a man to completely miss the important things in life. "There were many opportunities, darling. She chose not to take them."

"She has a great deal on her mind."

"She has nothing on her mind except that ridiculous inn."

He gave her the patented blue-eyed look that had been turning her emotions inside out from the day they first met in the lobby of the Carillon. "If memory serves, she was rather vehement on the subject of things romantic."

"Oh, she's just tired of her mother-in-law's match-making." She sidestepped with a casual wave of her hand. "I must say, however, that I noticed a definite change of mood when I came back from the ladies' room. She seemed rather pensive."

"It was your strawberry tart," he said, easing the Rolls to a stop at a traffic light. "She'd been contemplating taking it under house arrest."

"Good try." Holland tapped a Gauloise out of the packet resting on the console between them. "If you hadn't looked so serious when I sat down, I might believe you." Over the past two years, she'd become quite adept at noticing the unusual when it pertained to Alistair Chambers.

He pressed in the lighter, then held it to the tip of her cigarette. She nodded her thanks and drew in deeply on the pungent foreign blend.

How easy it was to grow accustomed to the finer things. Imported cigarettes. Rolls-Royces and Mercedes-Benzes with leather upholstery softer than a baby's behind. Impromptu trips to Bermuda where a yacht awaited milady's pleasure.

But, more than that—oh, God, so much more—how easy, how terrifyingly easy it was to grow accustomed to love. This man with his wit and charm and intelligence had managed to somehow get beneath her veneer of sophistication and find the heart she'd thought immune to such things.

When they'd first met, Holland had been prepared for a brief, but wonderful, interlude with a charming, urbane Englishman.

She hadn't been prepared for the many riddles and contradictions that were part and parcel of that charming, urbane Englishman.

Or for the surprise of falling in love.

The light changed to green, and Alistair turned onto the twisting mountain road that led back to Hideaway Haven. The silence in the car pressed against her chest and, with apologies to the surgeon general, she wondered how nonsmokers filled awkward moments such as this.

The Actor's Studio had long ago taught Holland one hundred and seventeen bits of business guaranteed to help an actor turn smoking into a social statement.

She was using at least three of them at the moment but, unfortunately, none of them seemed to be working. Maybe blunt talk would.

"My self-confidence isn't that shaky, darling," she said as they inched their way up the hill toward Hideaway Haven. "Sarah's name doesn't strike fear into my heart."

"May I ask what brought on that rather remarkable statement?"

She tilted her chin slightly and took a protracted drag on the Gauloise. "I would think it perfectly obvious."

He laughed for the first time since they had left the Bronze Penguin. "My love, with you nothing on earth is perfectly obvious."

*You fool,* she thought. *Don't you see my heart on my sleeve?* "Sarah was your wife. She was Maggie's aunt. It's perfectly normal to speak about her from time to time." *And perfectly normal for me to feel threatened.*

He slowed the Rolls down and eased it into a particularly nasty curve. "And that's what you believe we were talking about this afternoon?"

Her shoulders lifted in a shrug as she flicked her cigarette. Even the ashtrays in a Rolls were first-class. "What else could it be?" She'd only seen that vulnerable look on his face when Sarah McBride Chambers's name had been mentioned.

"I apologize if we made you uncomfortable. It was unintentional."

"I know." She wished she'd never started this whole miserable conversation. For two years now, she'd been finding herself up against one locked door after another. Not even her best friend, Joanna, who had married Alistair's protégé, Ryder O'Neal, was able to shed any light on this man she loved. "I know you have a past, Alistair. I wouldn't wish otherwise." A pause, well-timed and sharpened from years of practice. "Certainly I have one of my own."

Alistair, however, didn't rise to the bait. He merely switched on the stereo, but not even the beautiful strains of Mozart could hide the ugly truth.

*Grow up, woman,* she thought as she watched the stands of pine roll past her window. *Understand what's going on here.*

This was the 1980s, not the turn of the century. She didn't need a man to make her life complete. Once she'd believed she would give up her career for the love of a man.

That, of course, was before she had a career to speak of.

Alistair kept huge parts of his life excruciatingly private. Even in their most intimate moments, she felt as if she touched only a fraction of the man he really was. That maddening British reserve kept him safely out of reach.

She'd managed to make many of her own dreams come true without fairy godmothers or sugar daddies or pacts with the devil.

She was a fiercely independent forty-four-year-old woman who'd gotten along just fine without Alistair Chambers and would get along just fine again when Alistair Chambers was but a pleasant memory to warm her by a fire.

She stubbed out the half-smoked Gauloise and stared out the window at the acres of woodland whizzing by.

*I love you,* she thought.

But no one had ever said love was enough in a dangerous age. Maybe Maggie was right: steer clear of romantic entanglements, and concentrate only on the things you can control.

And, God knew, she couldn't control Alistair Chambers. She couldn't even understand him. He said he was a financier, but financiers didn't disappear for weeks on end or vanish in the dark of night without explanation.

"Take him on faith," Joanna had said. "Trust him. He'll never hurt you."

Holland had been trying it now for two long years, and it was taking its toll on her.

It had been wonderful, but the signs were unmistakable.

She loved him, but she was going to make sure she was the first to say goodbye.

# Chapter Four

There was definitely something to be said for being understaffed, Maggie thought as she propped her feet up on the front porch railing and settled back to watch another Poconos sunset.

Normally the sight of the indigo and violet streaks of color blossoming in the western sky triggered memories of sunsets from other times, other places.

The soft night air of Caracas. The savage splendor of fjords near Stockholm. The old thrill of living day-to-day.

Everything she'd tossed aside when she married Richard Douglass.

When you were functioning as owner, manager, part-time chef and full-time social director, there wasn't much time left at the end of the day to spend mooning over anything beyond the next day's breakfast menu.

Tonight, however, was different.

Breakfast menus and Friday night's costume party were far from her mind. Even the amazing fact that she'd saved the life of one John Adams Tyler ran a poor second to the memory of how her entire body had flamed to life from the second she saw him walk into the Bronze Penguin.

If it wasn't for the fact that she'd given key members of her staff the month of August off, Maggie might have stretched out on the porch, hours earlier, nursing a cold lemonade and a few steamy fantasies.

Plain ordinary exhaustion made it hard to nurse fantasies any more exciting than the dream of ten hours of unbroken sleep and a No Vacancy sign twinkling merrily overhead.

God knew, she was doing her best to make it all work just the way she and Rick had wanted it to, back in the beginning. Two months ago she'd hocked a pair of gold hoop earrings—bought a lifetime ago when she was on assignment in Cairo—and plunked the money down on a full-color ad in *Modern Bride* calculated to lure hundreds of honeymooners to the one classy establishment west of the Delaware Water Gap.

So much for class.

August was limping toward September, and she had enough empty rooms to hold a Shriners convention.

The White Elephant had been Rick's dream, his baby. In the beginning her involvement had been strictly out of loyalty: first, to help her husband; then to preserve his memory.

But it was more than that to her now. She genuinely loved the hotel business, loved the challenge of turning something as down on its luck as The White Elephant into a rousing success.

Perhaps that was why her work with PAX had never been as important to her as Alistair and Sarah would have liked.

PAX was an elite organization that prided itself on excellence.

It had to.

On more occasions than Maggie sometimes liked to remember, the lives of millions of innocent people had hung in the balance, and only swift action on the part of PAX members had saved them.

Being part of the organization had been heady stuff for a young girl barely out of school. The travel, the challenge, the danger had all been great fun for a while.

Cryptography to Maggie was like working on a giant-sized crossword puzzle from *The New York Times* in ink. Only difference was, one wrong answer and a government could topple.

She'd come by her gift for esoteric electronic wizardry naturally, a direct result of the McBride blood that flowed through her veins. When her parents had died during her senior year in high school, Sarah and Alistair had opened their doors and their hearts to her, and she'd fallen into the "family business" as easily as if that business had been dry cleaning or dressmaking.

Nice work if you could get it.

But the commitment hadn't been there. Instead she found herself bound by a combination of talent and loyalty, and it wasn't until love, in the form of Rick Douglass, came along that she realized the extraordinary life of an operative wasn't for her.

PAX didn't need her; Rick Douglass did.

Maggie had always championed the underdog, and there wasn't a bigger underdog in the world than The White Elephant.

She reached for the lemonade resting by her chair and winced as drops of condensation landed on her bare legs.

"Such pastoral splendor! It's enough to make a man rethink the progress of the twentieth century."

There on the top step stood her Uncle Alistair, nattily attired in white duck pants, starched shirt and blue blazer complete with crest. The only thing missing was the yacht, and that, if she remembered right, was moored at the moment in Bermuda.

She motioned for him to pull up a chair. "So the city dweller discovers rural bliss. Better be careful, Alistair. Country living can be addictive."

Her uncle lowered his well-tailored frame into a huge wicker club chair and poured himself some lemonade from the pitcher on the side table.

"Ah, yes!" He looked out at the expanse of lawn that sloped gently down to a garden of late summer flowers as a crackling noise mingled with the chirp of crickets. "The romantic sound of a family of mosquitoes meeting their Maker. How can the New York Philharmonic ever compete?"

"If you lived here year-round, you'd know the sound of a good bug zapper is better than Mozart."

"A wealth of culture," he said, arching a brow in her direction. "How have I survived so long without it?"

"You old snob." Maggie's voice was filled with affection. "Where's your pioneering spirit?"

"I'm English. We leave pioneering to you upstart Colonials."

"Look at that sunset. You don't find sunsets like that in Manhattan."

"And you don't find *Les Misérables* in East Point."

"Give us five or ten years," she said, laughing. "I'm sure the road company will find us."

He glanced around at The White Elephant with its peeling paint and overgrown lawn. "Or one of your competitors."

"Speaking of my competitors, how did you manage to tear yourself away from the pleasure palace long enough to visit us simple folk?"

"Holland is performing one of those eminently secret rituals understood only by the female of the species, and it occurred to me this was the perfect time to visit my beloved niece."

Maggie gave the East Point version of the Bronx cheer. "You'll have to do better than that."

"I thought that was a fairly accurate assessment of my intentions."

"You may fool others with that British charm, but I'm immune, Ally," she said good-naturedly. "I know you too well. You're here for a reason, and it's not The White Elephant's lemonade."

"You seem rather tense tonight, Maggie."

She sighed and rested her empty lemonade glass on the porch railing. "I'm overtired and overworked."

"What you need is a vacation."

"That's what Rachel and George keep telling me." Her in-laws had been engaged in a long-standing campaign to get Maggie rested and remarried. "They want me to spend a month with them in Scandinavia this fall."

"You've seen Scandinavia many times."

"This has nothing to do with sight-seeing, uncle mine."

"Matchmaking again?"

"What else? They probably figure they can pass an international smorgasbord under my nose, and I'll have to pick at least one appetizer."

Alistair lit a Gauloise and inhaled deeply. "The third week of September seems a perfect time for a getaway."

The tip of his cigarette glowed orange in the gathering darkness, and apprehension suddenly coiled inside Maggie's stomach.

"What are you driving at?" *I've left the organization behind me. I don't need it anymore.*

"You have the third week of September empty."

"Oh, no, you don't. I'm retired, Alistair. Can't you leave PAX back in the real world? I don't want it here." *You know I can't refuse you.*

He leaned forward, and even in the gathering twilight the look in his eyes was unmistakable.

"I have a proposition for you, Magdalena."

She leaned back and took a long sip of lemonade before answering. "I'm not interested."

"PAX needs your help."

Her heart slammed against her rib cage as a decade of memories rushed in. "I'm definitely not interested."

"At least hear me out before you decline."

She swung her feet down from the porch railing and stood up. "I'm not going back in, Alistair. I gave up that life a long time ago, and I don't—" She stopped and stared at him. "Would you mind telling me why in hell you're laughing?"

"I don't recall asking you to rejoin the organization."

"When you said you had a proposition, I assumed—"

He raised his hand to silence her. "I respect your feelings totally."

She towered over him, hands planted on her hips. The body-language battle was one she intended to win. "What is it you want from me?"

"Take a seat."

"And give you the advantage?" She shook her head. "I'll stand, thank you."

"As you wish." He lit another cigarette.

"Go ahead and make your pitch, Alistair, if that's what will make you happy, but I'm telling you in advance you won't change my mind." If it hadn't been Rick Douglass, it would have been something else. The nomadic life of an operative had never been the life for her.

"Dear girl, once more you're jumping to conclusions."

"You don't need me for some special assignment?" She still carried one of the highest security clearances granted to civilians, tribute to the McBride gift that had manifested itself in her almost preternatural talent for cryptography. For five years she had worked side by side with some of the most talented people in the Western world, her Aunt Sarah included.

"Sorry to disappoint you, but no special assignment."

To hell with body language. Maggie sank down onto the edge of her chair. "I don't get it."

"We want The White Elephant, and we're willing to compensate you handsomely for the privilege."

Privilege? In the same sentence as The White Elephant? She must be going crazy.

"You want the inn?"

He nodded.

"The inn and not me?"

"You can take my boat out. Charles has it ready in Bermuda. Just say the word, and the vacation is on the organization."

"And I suppose you can suggest just when I should take this vacation?"

"But, of course. September nineteenth through September twenty-fifth." How clever of him. It coincided with Rachel's vacation, as well.

"Forget it," she said. "I'm expecting heavy traffic in September."

"As of this moment, that week is still unscheduled."

Her face flamed, and she thanked God for twilight. "It's only a matter of time. My advertisement just ran in *Modern Bride* and I know it will—"

"It won't."

"Of course it will. It's a four-color, full-page ad, Alistair. If that doesn't bring in business I'll eat my—"

"Your ad didn't run, my dear girl."

"What is this, *The Twilight Zone*? I have a copy in my office." She headed toward the door. "I'll show you."

She stormed through the cool foyer, with Alistair following behind. She didn't even notice the shimmering parquet floor she'd hocked her Rolex for, or the antique registration desk that had once been a classic Mustang V-8. A shoulder-high stack of boxes partially blocked the opening to her office, and she neatly vaulted over them.

"What is all this?" Alistair sidestepped the obstruction. "The deluge of reservations you were expecting?"

"Cocktail napkins," she said, rummaging through the accumulation of mail on her desk. "A year's supply—ah-hah! Here it is!" She waved a shiny magazine page aloft. "Read it and weep, Ally. My full-page ad, *Modern Bride*, July issue."

He scanned it briefly, then handed it back to her. "Joanna did a wonderful job, didn't she?"

"Joanna?"

"Ryder's wife. You *do* remember Ryder O'Neal, don't you?"

"Of course I remember Ryder." Ryder, one of the best operatives the organization had ever known, was the son Alistair and Sarah never had, and Maggie had been lucky enough to share a number of fascinating cases with him during her years at PAX. "His wife works for *Modern Bride*?"

Alistair's laugh filled the room. "Joanna works for us, dear girl. That ad you're clutching is her handiwork."

"Are you telling me I've been set up?"

"Such an ugly phrase."

Maggie sagged against the edge of her desk. "The ad didn't run," she murmured. "September will be worse than August."

At least Alistair had the grace to look sympathetic. Not that it mattered, though. She still wanted to give him a good right hook.

"There's still my offer to consider, Maggie. You stand to be handsomely rewarded."

He named a figure that would easily pull The White Elephant into the middle of the next year, with cash to spare.

"Why The White Elephant? Is it our high ceilings? Our sprawling grounds? Our fine cuisine?" The secret passageways Tyler was so curious about? What could be better for a group of spies looking for a place to hide?

Alistair looked uncomfortable. "I can see there is to be no easy way to break this to you. We want The White Elephant because nobody knows it exists."

"Whatever happened to cushioning a blow?"

"You asked for honesty."

"Honesty, yes. Brutality, no." She took another look at the ad copy that had totally fooled her. "I was in the business. I shouldn't have been taken in like this."

He laughed. "Joanna is a wizard, isn't she? Expensive, but worth every shilling."

Alistair repeated his dollar offer.

"Should you say no, that should compensate you for any inconvenience."

Compensate her? It was more than she'd made in the past two years combined.

"And what if I say yes? You'll be putting me out of business for a full week." How she ever managed to get that out with a straight face was beyond her.

How Alistair managed not to laugh out loud was beyond comprehension. His next figure was double the one before. Maggie began to salivate.

"What's the catch?" There had to be one. Not even the almighty PAX made offers this good without a catch.

"How suspicious you are, my girl. All you need do is go off and enjoy yourself for a few days, and when you come back, The White Elephant will be on the front page of every newspaper in the world."

"I'm waiting. What's the story?"

"I'm not at liberty to discuss the details until we have come to an accord."

"Does it involve bloodshed?"

He said nothing.

"Murder?"

Still nothing.

"An exchange of identities?"

He shook his head. "You should know better, Maggie. I'll tell you nothing until we have an agreement."

"And I won't agree until you tell me something."

"Then we appear to be at an impasse."

They stared at each other for a full minute, two old warriors in friendly competition.

Alistair, to Maggie's intense surprise, was the first one to crack.

"I'll go up another twenty percent, but that's it, Magdalena. Any more than that, and I'll take my business to Hideaway Haven."

"You really know how to hurt a person, don't you, Ally?"

"Take it or leave it, my girl. This is my last offer."

It was already late August.

*Very* late August.

There was no way on earth any other hotel, motel or inn could possibly accommodate the organization with so little notice.

There was also no way on earth she could turn away from money of the magnitude Alistair was offering.

"You drive a hard bargain," she said, fingering the ledger resting atop her desk. "My old loyalties to PAX run deep."

He stared at her for a moment, then burst out laughing. "Careful, my girl, your greed is showing."

"I wish you wouldn't be so blunt, Ally. Where's your finesse?"

"Finesse? We've been through too much over the years for finesse."

She repeated the last figure plus an additional five percent. "Agreed?"

His eyebrow arched. He cut it by two and a half. "Agreed?"

"You drive a hard bargain, uncle mine." She extended her right hand. "You've got a deal."

She poured them each a sherry from the decanter on the credenza by the window.

"To PAX," said Alistair, raising his glass.

"To a new central heating unit and a ski lift," said Maggie, taking a sip. "I can't wait to tell Rachel about the windfall."

Alistair put his glass down on the filing cabinet. "That brings me to the one unpleasant detail."

She groaned. "I knew this was too good to be true."

"A minor detail. I want you to keep an extremely low profile until after the Summit Meeting."

Maggie's jaw came unhinged. "Summit Meeting!" A sudden absurd image of the president and the Russian secretary shaking hands on the Kissing Bridge sprang to life. "At The White Elephant?"

Her uncle grinned at her. "Incredible, isn't it?" He quickly outlined the Summit Meeting of the reigning superpowers, aimed at taking another step toward nuclear disarmament. "Your inn will be world famous one month from now."

Another absurd image, this time of the First Lady dining off mismatched china, loomed ahead. "I don't have enough dinner plates."

"The president's staff will supply everything."

"The carpets," Maggie sputtered. "The cracks in the driveway, the way the roof—"

"It will all be corrected."

She felt as if she were Dorothy in the tornado spinning her way to Oz. "All that and money, too?" She glanced behind her. "Are you sure Mephistopheles isn't lurking somewhere? *Glasnost* never looked so good."

"Accept your good fortune gracefully, Magdalena. It's long overdue."

She tossed a paper clip at him. "And all I have to do is keep my mouth shut until I leave for a week in Bermuda?"

"Simply keep your name out of the newspapers, beware of strangers bearing gifts, and accept no new business until it's all over."

"It's going to be tough," she said dryly. "After September fifteenth, my guest book is clear into the next millennium, and the last stranger to give me a gift was our local Avon lady. You'd be surprised how wonderful their waterproof mascara is."

"And the newspapers?" he asked, laughing. "Can you manage to stay out of the headlines?"

"'A lady's name appears in the newspaper but three times in her life: at birth, upon her marriage and in death.'" Maggie's smile was rueful. "Grandma McBride would be proud of me."

Alistair refilled their glasses. "To Grandma McBride," he said, "and to other ladies of breeding."

Maggie thought of the glorious headlines that would be splashed around the world in just one month.

"To free publicity," she said. "The cornerstone of our capitalist system."

"Remember Grandma McBride," Alistair warned. "She also said, 'Good things come to those who wait.'"

One last vision flared to life: Barbara Walters sitting on the chintz-covered divan in Maggie's parlor interviewing her while, outside shivering in the snow, Dan Rather, Tom Brokaw and Peter Jennings vied for a moment of her time.

"Don't worry," she said confidently. "Short of running naked through East Point, there's nothing I could do to end up in the papers."

But in thirty days?

Watch out!

## Chapter Five

Maybe it was indicative of the foolishness of old age, but Alistair Chambers didn't feel the slightest bit embarrassed as he steered the Rolls-Royce up the heart-shaped driveway leading to Love Cottage, Number 9 after leaving Maggie that night.

He'd hobnobbed with kings and queens in marble-and-gilt drawing rooms.

He'd dined with sheikhs and concubines in palaces of barbaric splendor.

He'd seen the Taj Mahal by moonlight and Paris at dusk, but he'd never seen anything more beautiful than this.

The electric candle in the window twinkled in the dark Pennsylvania night, and for a moment it called to mind other nights in other places when the woman waiting for him had been a part of the setting, but not part of his heart.

He couldn't even pinpoint when it had happened, the exact moment when Holland Masters stopped being delightful company and became something more.

The empty aching void Sarah's death had left inside his soul hurt less with each day. Sunsets were more beautiful, music more poignant, each hour more filled with promise than the hour before.

The sweetness of life flowed over him, bathing him in honey, urging him forward, toward a place he thought never to see again.

*Love.*

He was in love.

Alistair Chambers loved Holland Masters with a passion and fervor and intensity that breathed optimism and youth into his tired, jaded heart.

He'd watched it happen to his young protégé, Ryder O'Neal, and he'd rejoiced when Ryder and Joanna married in a blaze of romantic glory. They'd managed to combine forces and share a very difficult way of life much the same as he and Sarah had managed to combine their marriage with their commitment to PAX.

A man couldn't be twice blessed.

And therein rested the problem.

Holland was at the top of her profession. Twenty years of hard work had finally paid off, and she was enjoying the success that had long eluded her. Her life was filled with excitement and glamour, and the uncompromising glare of the spotlight—the one thing he'd avoided all his adult life.

He was running out of excuses, Alistair was.

He'd managed to be out of town when the daytime Emmys were given out.

He'd been away on business when the cast of *Destiny* held its Christmas party.

A rash of oddly timed bouts with the flu had kept him from dinner parties and weddings and weekends on Long Island with her friends.

Except for occasional dinners with Ryder and Joanna in out-of-the-way restaurants, their entire courtship had been conducted in private.

He pulled the Rolls-Royce into the parking lot in front of their cottage and turned off the engine, filling the car with the sound of country silence. The persistent buzz of the crickets was broken only by the angry crackle of a hungry bug zapper somewhere in the distance.

Looking up at the sky, his eyes automatically sought Polaris, the North Star. How many times in how many places had Polaris been the one constant guiding him home?

Polaris couldn't help him this time, though. The brightest star on his horizon now was Holland Masters.

Even here, tucked away in the heart of the Pocono Mountains, there'd been the shy looks of recognition, the requests for autographs, the current of excitement that seemed to follow her every move.

"Damn it to bloody hell!" he said into the darkness.

She needed more.

She needed a man who could stand beside her and share in her happiness.

What she didn't need was an aging warrior who lingered in the shadows because it had been so damned long since he'd faced the daylight.

Three years ago he had laughed at Ryder and the younger man's yearning to break free of PAX and build a life of his own. He'd done everything in his power to keep Ryder tied in with the organization, certain that duty and happiness were indivisible, that fulfillment lay in serving a higher cause.

Fate had been kinder to Ryder than Alistair, and had brought him a woman who could share the adventure.

Fate hadn't been as kind to Alistair and Holland.

The signs had been there for a long time, but he'd been too much in love to see. Selfishly he'd turned a blind eye to everything but his need for her. She'd become a part of his life so quickly, so completely, that now he wondered how he would ever live without her.

Inside Love Cottage, Number 9, Holland slept by the light of the dying fire, her black negligee soft as a whisper against her skin.

He knew that if he truly loved her, he would have to let her go.

But as he lay down next to her and drew her into his arms, he knew that leaving would break his heart.


MAGGIE WAS JUST BEGINNING the madhouse known as the breakfast rush the next morning when her mother-in-law, Rachel Douglass, burst into the kitchen of The White Elephant waving a copy of the *Pocono Bugle* overhead like a banner.

"Page one, column one!" Rachel crowed triumphantly while Maggie stopped four eggs from crashing to the tiled floor. "Free publicity, and you're a hero to boot." She gave Maggie an exuberant hug. "Honey, this kind of coverage is worth its weight in gold bullion."

Maggie extricated herself from the hug and wiped her butter- and bacon-stained hands on her apron. Rachel's words had tumbled over one another so quickly that Maggie needed a translator.

"Whoa!" she said, laughing. "Slow it down, Rachel. I didn't understand a word you said." Then it hit her. "Did you say free publicity?"

"I knew that would get you." Rachel thrust the newspaper into Maggie's hands. "Read it and see. I must say that's some picture of you, honey."

"At last! I've been waiting six months for my publicity photo to run," Maggie said, spreading the newspaper out on the counter. "After all the business I've tossed to Kraemer at the *Bugle*, it's about time he— Oh, my God!"

It wasn't her publicity photo.

What it was, was scandalous. An old-fashioned word, maybe, but there was no other way to describe it.

There, for the entire world to see, was a prone John Adams Tyler on the floor of the Bronze Penguin with a very agile Maggie sitting astride him with her skirt hiked up well beyond the comfort zone.

Maggie buried her head in her hands. "I'm humiliated."

"Because you're showing a bit of thigh?" Rachel laughed and ruffled Maggie's hair. "We're on the verge of the twenty-first century, honey."

"Look at this!" Maggie said, pointing at the picture. "I look like I'm enjoying myself."

"What's not to enjoy? He's a gorgeous man, not Quasimodo. If George wasn't the jealous sort, I wouldn't mind posing for a picture myself."

Rachel's eyes gleamed with mischief, and Maggie gave her a swat with a dish towel. "I was saving his life, Rachel, not seducing him. This picture makes it look like something it wasn't."

"Spare me the details," her mother-in-law said, cupping her hands over her ears. "Let me dream."

Maggie tried to scan the article, but her eyes were drawn repeatedly to the black-and-white photo on the center of the front page.

Damn, but she could still feel the soft scratch of his perfectly pressed pants against her inner thighs, the heat of his flesh when she rested her cheek against his chest.

Forget the reality of Chicken Kiev and competition. The photo was blatantly sexy, and she found it difficult to look at it and breathe at the same time.

If Maggie, who was one-half of that extremely cozy couple, felt that way, what on earth was everyone else in the Poconos thinking?

"Margo Wayne will have a field day with this," she said, turning the paper over so she could think. "She'll probably pass this around as a handout at the next hotel owners' meeting."

"Margo Wayne is a dried-up old prune with iced water in her veins."

Maggie looked at her mother-in-law and laughed out loud. "Margo Wayne is forty-two years old, five times married and busier than Joan Collins."

She had to hand it to Rachel. The truth didn't faze her at all. "Who cares what Margo or any of them has to say? This is the best free publicity for The White Elephant that I've ever seen. I wouldn't be surprised if it ends up in next week's *People* magazine."

*People* magazine? That was national exposure on a scale that even *Modern Bride* couldn't compete with. The full-page ad that had cost her her Egyptian earrings wouldn't reach one-tenth of—

Alistair.

The *Modern Bride* ad that really wasn't.

Her promise to keep a low profile until after the Summit Meeting.

"He's going to kill me."

Rachel's pale blond brows lifted. "Who's going to kill you?"

"Alistair."

"Your uncle?"

Obviously when she'd left PAX she'd also left behind her talent for discretion. "He, um, he hates to take a back seat to anyone." She picked up the *Pocono Bugle* and scanned the article again. "See? They didn't mention him once." At least she hadn't lost her facility for covering her tracks.

Rachel didn't look convinced. "I would have figured Holland for the publicity hound. Your uncle seems more the understated type."

"Looks can be deceiving," Maggie said with a shrug. When in doubt, reach for a cliché.

"What an interesting turn of phrase," her mother-in-law said dryly. "May I quote you on that?"

"Come on, Rae, it's early. You know I never come up with original material before noon."

"Excuses, excuses," Rachel said. "Why don't you—"

Angie, one of the waitresses, popped up in the kitchen doorway. "They're starting to eat the flower arrangements," she said, grabbing a slice of toast from the counter near the door. "Where's the food?"

Maggie pushed a tray of strawberry-filled cantaloupe halves toward the young girl. "Here, feed them this." She glared at her mother-in-law. "I thought you said honeymooners had other things on their minds."

"They did in my day," Rachel said, manning the huge, twelve-square waffle iron. "I don't know what's becoming of this younger generation."

Maggie, who had a few ideas of her own on that subject, kept them to herself. There were omelets to make, hash browns to fry and a thousand excuses to come up with before Alistair saw the front page of the *Pocono Bugle*.

THE DELIVERY BOY STOOD in the center of John Tyler's office and stared at the stack of boxes piled up and ready to go.

"Let me see if I've got it," he said, scratching his head with the tip of his pencil. "I deliver 'em. You follow me."

"You got it," said John, signing the invoice. "Not so hard, is it?"

"Never said it was hard. It's *weird* is what it is."

John's assistant, Shawna Campbell, stifled a laugh, and he shot her a dirty look.

"Don't worry about it," he said. "Everything's on the up-and-up."

The kid still looked suspicious. "This isn't some kind of test, is it? I do my job right, and I don't need nobody checking up on me."

"This hasn't one damned thing to do with you."

The kid shrugged and headed for the door. "Suit yourself. I got another delivery to make before yours, so let's get moving."

John saluted the boy's skinny back as he followed him outside. "Damn kid isn't even dry behind the ears yet," he said in amazement. "He tosses off orders better than I do."

"I noticed," said Shawna dryly. "Better watch it. Your soft heart is showing."

*She's right,* he thought as he headed for his car.

Normally he could buy and sell ten million dollars' worth of property and not blink an eye.

Yet there he was, fumbling to get his key into the ignition of the Jaguar and praying his Right Guard had the right stuff.

Love, he thought as he eased the car out onto the main road.

The older you get, the harder you fall.

The White Elephant—next right.

He was getting older by the minute.

"SOMEDAY..." MAGGIE MUMBLED two hours later as she faced a roomful of dirty pans, filthy pots, egg-encrusted dishes and lipstick-smeared glassware. "Someday..."

Rachel brushed back a lock of pale blond hair and continued rewrapping a Virginia ham the size of an underdeveloped nation. "Don't tell me," she said, reaching for another square of plastic wrap, "let me guess. Someday you'll learn not to give the kitchen crew the month of August off."

"I had to give them August off," said Maggie, scraping plates into the garbage disposal. "I couldn't afford to pay them."

"You should have at least hired a temporary cook." Rachel eyed the remnants of an aborted breakfast quiche. "In case you haven't noticed, honey, we're not exactly Julia Child."

"No one stormed the kitchen," Maggie pointed out.

"They didn't have the energy. They were weak with hunger."

Maggie picked up the huge carving knife she'd used to slice the ham. "I was ready for them." The blade whistled through the air as she carved an imaginary X. "I'm nothing if not resourceful."

"I must say I'd never noticed you had such a knack with knives. We could have used you at Thanksgiving dinner last year."

Maggie laughed and put the knife into the dishwasher. "And deprive the Douglass men of their biological rights? Perish the thought."

"They do take it seriously, don't they?" Rachel mused. "I'm almost afraid to consider the psychological ramifications. Some swashbuckling Scotsman in their background.''

Rachel's bawdy chatter about Errol Flynn and the obvious merits of pirate movies starring men in waist-slashed shirts kept Maggie laughing, and before she knew it, the kitchen was in order.

''Terrific,'' Maggie said, glancing up at the huge clock hanging over the double sink. ''Just twenty minutes until they start clamoring for lunch.''

''Ah, yes.'' Rachel untied her apron and tossed it into the basket near the door to the laundry room. ''Amazing what a ruckus twelve hungry newlyweds can make.''

Ten hungry newlyweds, thought Maggie. Not that she was counting.

''It's the slow season, Rachel. Business will pick up in September.'' She bit back a smile. After the publicity surrounding the Summit Meeting, she should be doing turn-away business.

''Have you driven past Hideaway Haven lately?'' Rachel, who liked to live dangerously, asked. ''Business isn't slow up there.''

''I'm getting sick to death of hearing about Hideaway Haven! First Alistair throws it in my face, then Holland, and now you.'' She tossed her own apron into the basket and reached for a clean one. ''Would you tell me how the Poconos ever managed to get along before that bastion of bad taste opened?''

''Competition is good for the economy.''

''Not for *my* economy, it isn't. Do you know he actually bribed Claude for the best seat in the house?''

''My kind of man,'' said Rachel. ''He knows what he wants and he's not afraid to buy it.'' She picked up the *Pocono Bugle* from the counter and let out a long, slow whistle. ''Is he really this gorgeous?'' Rachel, forty years married and still in love with her husband, feigned a swoon over the top of the dishwasher. "He's the talk of the beauty shop. Alice says he's the best thing to come along since Tom Selleck."

Alice Niedermeyer had owned the beauty shop in town for over a quarter century and had her Clairol-covered finger on the pulse of all that happened within a ten-mile radius.

"He's attractive enough, I guess. I really didn't pay that much attention to him." Maggie was amazed her nose didn't grow a yard after a whopper like that one.

Rachel, wise woman that she was, wasn't buying any of it. "You can tell me, honey." She fixed Maggie with a look whose meaning she knew all too well. "No one on earth wants to see you happy more than I do."

"You really want to see me happy?"

"Of course," said Rachel.

Maggie picked up another clean apron and tossed it at her mother-in-law. "Then help me with lunch."

"Sorry, honey," Rachel said, grabbing her pocketbook from the hook inside the pantry closet, "but I have an appointment with Alice, and dark roots wait for no woman."

"You're a traitor, Rachel Douglass!" Maggie called out as her mother-in-law disappeared out the back door. "A traitor!"

Alistair was bound to pop up any minute, filled with righteous indignation and British hellfire, and Maggie had been banking on her mother-in-law's considerable charm to take some of the heat off her.

She leaned against the dishwasher and took another look—a long one this time—at the picture on the front page of the *Bugle*.

Unless she missed her guess, Rachel was dead-on. This was exactly the kind of picture that went whizzing through the wire services to all the people-watching magazines hungry for new faces.

She could see that Olympic-sized heated swimming pool going up in smoke before her very eyes.

Damn it! Alistair had been there at the Bronze Penguin. He'd seen the whole thing happen. He'd even been the one to call 911 when they still believed Tyler was having a heart attack right there on the floor.

So what if she got a little bit of publicity? There certainly wouldn't be an instant replay of the situation between now and the Summit Meeting. After all, how many men's lives did you save in an average month in East Point, Pennsylvania?

By tonight the excitement would be over, and she and The White Elephant could sink gracefully back into the obscurity to which they had become accustomed and bide their collective time.

No more front-page photos.

No more publicity.

No mysterious strangers bearing gifts or romantic entanglements.

The sound of car tires crunching through the loose gravel of her employees' parking lot could be heard through the kitchen window, followed by the thud of footsteps climbing the stairs.

Alistair certainly hadn't wasted time. She'd expected to have at least until midafternoon to put together her defense.

Well, if he wanted The White Elephant as much as she expected he did, he'd just have to look the other way.

After all, didn't today's news line the bottom of tomorrow's bird cage? It wouldn't be long before she and the gorgeous Mr. Tyler were staring up at Groucho from the bottom of his chrome-and-plastic split-level.

She opened the back door and, instead of her aristocratic uncle, she found herself looking into the face of the lanky delivery boy from one of the local courier offices.

"Shipment for you, Ms. Douglass." He pointed toward a stack of four huge boxes resting on the redwood porch.

"If this is apple-cinnamon bubble bath, you can just send it right back to Margo Wayne and—"

The delivery boy thrust a clipboard at her chest. "Sign here."

She grabbed his Bic pen and scribbled her name. "This *is* from Margo Wayne, isn't it?" It was just like Margo to pull a grandstand stunt like this—especially after that photo in the *Bugle*.

The boy shrugged and jammed the ballpoint back into his ink-stained shirt pocket. "I just deliver 'em," he said, looking strangely uneasy. "I don't ask no questions."

He bolted down the steps and roared off in his battered van before she could ask to see his shipping order.

She could just imagine Margo and Ernie and the rest of them sitting at breakfast that morning, having a good laugh over this. They probably expected her to send the packets of bubble bath flying right back to them by return courier along with an outraged note.

"You're in for a surprise this time, guys," she muttered as she tore off the heavy brown paper. Tonight when the lights were off and their swimming pools were empty, she'd—

This time the surprise was on her.

The boxes were filled with money.

# Chapter Six

A weaker woman might have fainted dead away at the sight of that king's ransom in twenty-dollar bills, but not Maggie Douglass.

Part of the McBride gift was an uncanny facility with numbers, and it took her all of two seconds to figure out that she was staring at over one million dollars.

Visions of a new guest wing and a private airstrip danced before her eyes like sugarplums at Christmas. She had to admit Alistair had really outdone himself this time. The Summit Meeting must mean a hell of a lot to PAX for her staid uncle to do something so extravagant, so totally out of character.

Holland's influence was more far-reaching than Maggie had ever imagined.

She pulled the buff-colored band from one stack of bills and savored the feel of them in her hand. Strange. Why hadn't she noticed before just how handsome Andrew Jackson was?

*Foolish woman!*

With that chiseled jawline and those eyes and that gorgeous head of dark hair—

Wait a minute.

Ol' Andy Jackson didn't have a gorgeous head of dark hair.

He didn't have a dimple just west of his mouth, or a lower lip so sexy it was just this side of perverse.

No, that wasn't the seventh president of the United States looking up at her from fifty-thousand oblong pieces of paper.

It was John Adams Tyler.

Her dream of a stable of full-time gardeners with a bouquet of green thumbs sputtered, then died, and to her utter amazement, Maggie began to laugh.

"I like that."

She turned in the direction of a masculine voice at the other end of the porch.

He spoke again. "It sounds promising."

John Adams Tyler, in the glorious flesh, was leaning against the railing, foot propped on the top step, watching her. He wore another Savile Row wonder, a sleek-fitting charcoal-gray suit her uncle would kill for. Another man would look ridiculous dressed like that in the middle of a Poconos summer.

He didn't.

And although *GQ* cover boys usually didn't do a thing for her, she suddenly wished she'd combed her hair and bothered with mascara and worn a bra beneath the clingy tank top that barely reached the waistband of her white shorts.

"I asked for a million dollars," she said, blessing the years with PAX where she'd learned to roll with the punches. "Should I count it, or can you be trusted?"

That aristocratic face of his broke into a surprisingly streetwise grin.

"I'd count it," he said, his hair glinting with amber highlights in the late-morning sun. "When it comes to money, it never hurts to double-check."

She examined one of the clever counterfeit bills. "Since these aren't exactly coin of the realm, I guess I can take your word for it."

He plucked a handful of fakes from the open box and riffled them like playing cards. "Had you going for a minute, didn't they?"

She dismissed the idea with a wave of her hand. "I wasn't fooled for a second."

"The hell you weren't. You'd spent half of it before I walked up the path."

The man was too perceptive. She opted for righteous indignation. "I value my privacy, Mr. Tyler. You should have let me know you were standing there."

"So you could put on your business face? No," he said, shaking his head, "this way was a lot more informative."

"So that's how you've clawed your way to the top, is it?" She folded one of the counterfeit bills and pushed it into the back pocket of her shorts. "No wonder you were able to renovate the Love Cottages in record time. When you're not spying on your competition, you're printing up your own capital in the basement."

A deep rolling laugh rumbled up from his impressively flat belly. "Keep it to yourself, will you? We're going public in a few weeks, and *Forbes* would have a field day with that."

She shook her head ruefully as her eyes flickered over the main building of The White Elephant. Two of the ruby-red shutters on the third floor dangled lopsidedly on their hinges, and great curls of faded white paint were peeling off the clapboard siding. "*Forbes* would put The

White Elephant on the endangered—'' She brought herself up short. "I must be crazy. You're the competition."

That streetwise grin reappeared. "I'm not worried if you're not."

"Is that an insult?"

"Perspective." He stepped closer. "It's all in how you look at things."

The perspective was obviously better when you were sitting on top of a multinational, multimillion-dollar enterprise, and Maggie was about to say so when Angie popped up at the back door.

"I can't find Rachel anywhere," the girl hollered, openly eyeing John. "Somebody'd better start the sloppy joes. They'll be comin' in from the bridle path any time."

"Sloppy joes?" He seemed to be having a tough time controlling his laughter.

"Perfectly legitimate meal. I suppose you serve pheasant under glass for lunch?"

Angie stepped out onto the porch before he had a chance to answer. "I'm not kiddin', Maggie. You better get started and fast."

"Damn," Maggie muttered under her breath. Rachel and her black roots! If Tyler hadn't been standing right there, enjoying every minute of her humiliation, she'd have picked up the phone and called Pizza Hut. Instead she said to Angie, "Get out the big iron skillets and the ground round. I'll be there in a minute."

Tyler waited until Angie had gone back inside. "Working the kitchen, are you? I thought you owned the place."

He already knew more facts and figures concerning her business than she did. What was a little more humiliation?

"I do own the place. That's why I work harder than anyone else."

"Puritan work ethic. Somehow you don't look the type."

Although there was nothing overtly sexual about the statement, she found herself aware of her body in a way she hadn't been a moment ago.

"Appearances can be deceiving. Who'd think someone like you would own old happy house?" She made a show of studying him. "I'd expect to see you playing the Bucks County country squire."

"Is that an insult?"

"Perspective." She tossed his words back at him. "Depends on how you look at it."

"Insult." He grinned at her, and she couldn't help grinning back. "I'll bet you think water beds are crass, and mirrored ceilings are a health hazard."

"Incredible. You read minds." She edged toward the back door. "I'd really love to stand out here and trade thoughts on the downfall of Western civilization, but I have to make lunch."

"Sloppy joes?"

"Sloppy joes."

"What about the money?" he asked.

"What about it? You had your laugh, now you can take it back with you."

"I want you to keep it."

"I don't think my bank would appreciate the deposit. You're cute, Mr. Tyler, but you're not Andrew Jackson."

"You could spend the money," he said, following her to the back door.

"Where? Disney World?"

"It's only good at Hideaway Haven."

She'd rather give it to Mickey Mouse and see him spend it on a two-year drinking binge. "Now I get it: The Club Med principle of entertainment."

"With a difference," he said, not batting an eyelash. "We're into monogamy."

"How interesting. One would think you'd be into whatever turned a profit."

"Pretty harsh judgment to make on such short acquaintance, Maggie Douglass."

"Your reputation precedes you, Mr. Tyler."

"So does yours."

"I was talking business."

He grinned. "So was I."

From inside, Angie's second call for help rang out loud and clear. "Take the money and run, Mr. Tyler, before I offer you Chicken Kiev."

She turned and stepped into the kitchen—with John right behind her.

"Persistent, aren't you?" she asked dryly as he shrugged out of his spiffy suit coat.

"That's how I got rich." He leaned back against one of the cabinets.

"You can make yourself comfortable," she said, "but don't expect me to make lunch for you." Ten hungry newlyweds were more than enough for one overworked inn owner to cope with.

"Who said anything about lunch?" He leaned over and hung his jacket from a hook near the pantry door.

"Who said anything about inviting you inside?" she countered. "You seem to take a lot for granted."

He looked around the empty kitchen. "You need help," he observed.

"I *have* help."

"They're either more well trained than Pavlov's dogs, or they all work the late shift."

"They're on vacation."

"The whole staff?"

She nodded.

"Bad planning, Maggie Douglass. No wonder you're in trouble over here."

"We're not in trouble over here. August is always slow. September is when we start to shine."

"Not according to my sources."

"To hell with your sources! I guarantee September will put The White Elephant on the map." *Shut up,* she warned herself. In another second, she'd be inviting him to the Summit Meeting.

"Will you still be pulling kitchen duty in September?"

"If that's your way of asking if I'll be fully staffed, the answer is yes." By presidents and prime ministers and more high-powered types than this guy had ever imagined.

How she'd love to tell him and watch his aristocratic jaw drop open in shock. Unfortunately she'd been too well trained for pleasures like that. No matter how difficult it was, she'd honor her promise to Alistair and bide her time until the third week of September, when The White Elephant would be on the lips of every newscaster from Minneapolis to Moscow.

She reached for a fresh apron and slipped it on over her tank top and shorts.

He unfastened his gold cuff links and rolled up his sleeves.

"Look," she said, "a joke's a joke. You've made your point. You can go home now."

"I thought I'd hang around for lunch. See what the competition is up to."

"Slumming, are you? Listen, I'm sick to death of Margo and Ernie and all the rest of you fat cats thumbing your noses at me. I have my own way of doing things, and I'll be damned if I'm going to—" She stopped dead in her tracks as Tyler opened her refrigerator, poked around and pulled out a fat Spanish onion. "What are you doing?"

"Making lunch." To her amazement, he started peeling the onion with quick efficient slashes of a paring knife.

"You don't owe me anything," she said, pulling three cans of Manwich out of the pantry.

"You saved my life," he said, rolling over her objections with the finesse of a bulldozer. "What kind of price do I put on that?"

"Eternal gratitude is enough." No shrines. No monuments. And definitely no help with lunch.

He ignored her and continued chopping.

The newspaper with that damning picture was faceup on the counter to his immediate left. He unnerved her enough standing there up to his elbows in Spanish onion. Vivid, tactile memories of his body beneath hers were wreaking havoc with her equilibrium.

Being in the same room with both him and that strangely erotic picture might be her undoing.

She tossed the ground round into the skillet and turned the flame up higher than her libido. Then she faced the enemy across the kitchen.

"Mr. Tyler—"

"John." His eyes twinkled with glimmers of topaz. She should have known a man like that wouldn't cry when he peeled an onion. Probably somewhere back at

Hideaway Haven, some lowly assistant's eyes were turning all red and watery as a favor to his boss. "It's a little late to stand on ceremony, isn't it, Maggie?"

Her thighs had been pressed against his hips less than twenty-four hours ago. She'd pressed her mouth to his bare chest. His skin had been warm and supple beneath her hands. Beads of sweat broke on the back of her neck.

If his body had felt that wonderful when he was unconscious, God only knew what would happen when he was— She cleared her throat. "Go home, John."     He stopped chopping. "What?"

"You're making me nervous." She grabbed the newspaper and thrust it behind her back. "When I'm nervous I can't cook."

"So don't cook. I'll do it."

"You don't seem to understand the problem here. You're the competition. I know all about the way you big-business types operate. You're supposed to be wishing financial ruin on me."

He was a better man than she. Maggie doubted if she'd have been able to ignore such a power-packed straight line, given the obvious shortcomings of The White Elephant.

"No hidden microphones," he said, patting his chest then turning his pants pockets inside out. He didn't even have lint. "No secret cameras." He picked up the paring knife again but pierced her with a look. "Besides, if you had anything I wanted here, you wouldn't be able to stop me. I always get what I want."

His words caused a flare of heat deep within her body. "An overstatement, I presume."

"No." His voice was low and intimate. "A statement of fact."

"Awfully sure of yourself, aren't you?"

"I don't believe in wasting time." His eyes never left hers. "I see what I want, and I zero in on it. A simple strategy, but effective."

"I would imagine so," she murmured. Her throat felt suddenly tight with emotions she'd relegated to her past, along with PAX and security clearances and the wedding band she once wore so proudly.

How she hated his type—so handsome, so privileged, so certain of his place in the world that it would never even occur to him that divine right wasn't a privilege granted to mortal men.

Strip him of that fancy suit and that swollen bank account, and you'd find a man struggling to find his place in the world.

Her type of man.

Lucky for Maggie that wasn't about to happen. He was the quintessential preppie prince and destined to remain so.

"You knew a great deal about The White Elephant," she said when she found her voice again.

"I know a great deal about all of my competitors. Especially the ones I try to buy out."

She took a step closer. "There isn't enough money in all of your Swiss bank accounts to get The White Elephant away from me."

He laughed, a marvelously primitive laugh. She wondered how many unsuspecting women had fallen prey to it.

"Don't worry," he said. "It's not The White Elephant I want. It's—"

"Am I interrupting something?"

Maggie wheeled around and saw Alistair in the doorway, his tanned forehead creased in a frown.

"Mr. Chambers." John raised the knife in salute. "I hope you and Ms. Masters are enjoying your stay with us."

"That we are," said Alistair. If he was surprised to see Tyler standing there in a gingham apron, he didn't let on. "We both dread the idea of leaving tonight."

Alistair was smiling, but Maggie knew the smile masked an anger that grew with each second. Damn it! Was nothing going right this morning?

"Perhaps you'll favor us with another, longer stay in the future," Tyler said smoothly.

Did he have to rub it in like that?

Maggie wanted nothing more than the pleasure of hitting him over the head with her iron skillet, but the thought of cleaning up the mess was sobering. If she hadn't given the kitchen staff the month off, Tyler would have been in big trouble.

"So, what brings you here, Uncle Alistair?"

Tyler's knife clattered to the counter. *"Uncle?"*

She ignored him and spoke to Alistair. "Are you here for lunch?" she persisted.

"Hardly that," said her uncle, the traitor, as he looked at the cans of Manwich lined up on the counter. "I understand we're dining on Shrimp de Jonghe this afternoon."

"Wimp food," she mumbled, reaching for the can opener. "Sloppy joes are classic American cuisine." When in doubt, brazen it out.

Not that anyone heard her. The two men were having a spirited discussion on food.

"The medallions of veal last night were superb," her uncle was saying. "Comparable to Le Cirque." He turned to Maggie. "Didn't I say that to you just last night?"

"Did you?" The can opener whirred. "I don't remember."

"I'm certain I did," Alistair went on, blithely unaware of her wrath. "I seem to recall mentioning it right after you told me about your rustlers' roundup buffet."

She glared at him. The rustlers' roundup was a White Elephant euphemism for "dinner is ruined, what the hell do we serve them now?"

John glanced from Alistair to Maggie, then rolled his sleeves back down and grabbed his jacket from the peg in the pantry. "I have a lunch meeting at one. I'd better get moving."

"So soon?" Alistair looked genuinely disappointed.

Maggie wanted to kick him in his elegant shins.

"My regards to Ms. Masters," he said, shaking Alistair's hand. "I hope you'll join us again soon."

"That, Mr. Tyler, is something you can count on."

Disgusting. The two of them were acting like reunited war buddies.

"Perhaps Mr. Tyler could give you a lift back to Hideaway Haven," Maggie said, piqued. "It's a terribly long walk from here, and I'd hate to overtire you."

"My pleasure," said Tyler. He had manners; she had to give him that.

"No need, Mr. Tyler. I brought the Rolls." The look he gave Maggie was something to behold. "My niece worries too much about my comfort."

"Well, you *are* getting on in years, Ally," she said sweetly as Tyler moved toward the door. "I'm just thinking of your welfare."

Alistair muttered one of the multilingual curses that had made him a legend at PAX, but Maggie just laughed and ushered Tyler onto the back porch.

"What did he say?" Tyler asked before the door squeaked behind them. "It sounded dirty."

"It was."

He looked at her curiously. "You understood him?"

"In a fashion," she said, "and after years of practice."

He tried to mimic the words Alistair had used, but became hopelessly tongue-tied. "What language was that anyway?"

She shrugged. "A little Greek, a little Latin—my uncle is a whiz with dead languages."

Tyler whistled low. "I'm impressed."

"He'll be thrilled. Alistair is a bit of a snob."

"What does he do anyway?"

"Do?"

"Career. A man like that must have a hell of a lot of stories to tell."

"That he has," she said carefully. "He's retired now."

"Retired from what?" Tyler didn't get where he was by giving up easily.

Butcher? Baker? Candlestick maker? Tyler would never buy the ordinary. "He's a retired polo player," she said finally. "World-class."

"Rich man's game," said Tyler. "Suits him."

"Are you leaving because Alistair showed up?"

"I told you I have a one-o'clock appointment."

"That didn't seem to bother you before my uncle dropped in."

"Let's just say I've decided to change my approach."

"Approach? What approach?"

"Have dinner with me tonight, and I'll explain it to you."

"The Bronze Penguin?" She made a mock shiver. "Do you dare?"

"I was thinking of Hideaway Haven."

"I'd rather go to McDonald's."

"Afraid of the competition are you, Maggie Douglass?"

"Competition doesn't faze me, Tyler. I'm afraid I'll choke on bad taste."

"Haven't you heard?" he said with a laugh. "The food's great. You can ask your uncle."

"It's not the food I'm worried about. You probably have smoked mirrors over the dining room tables and a heart-shaped dishwasher."

"Come for dinner and find out."

Her spirit was willing, but her flesh was embarrassingly weak. "If I do, will you consider your debt repaid?"

"It'll be a start."

"Tyler, I—"

He stopped her words with a kiss. It was only the slightest touch of his lips against hers, but it was enough to make her head spin with the touch and scent of him.

"Tonight," he said. "I'll pick you up at eight."

"Nine," she said, thinking of dinner for ten and the cleanup afterward. "I'll drive myself."

"Are you sure?"

"Positive."

"You don't trust me, do you?" He brushed her lower lip lightly with his index finger. The urge to draw it into her mouth and taste his flesh was overpowering.

"No," she whispered. "Not one damned bit."

But, even more frightening, for the first time in her life she didn't trust herself.

# Chapter Seven

Alistair was standing by the boxes of money when Maggie went back inside.

"Clever gimmick, isn't it?" She picked up a wooden spoon and stirred the sloppy joe mixture. "Just what you'd expect at the pleasure palace up there."

Alistair picked up a stack of bills and gave them a quick once-over. "May I ask what they're doing here at The White Elephant?"

She opened a huge white paper bag filled with hamburger buns from the bakery in town and arranged them on a cookie sheet so they could be warmed in the oven. "That's my reward for saving Tyler's life. Generous, isn't he?"

Alistair didn't crack a smile.

Maggie slid the rolls into the oven and turned to face the music.

"You saw the newspaper, didn't you?"

"I'm certain everyone in the Poconos saw the newspaper, Magdalena."

"He's photogenic, isn't he?"

"Quite. Unfortunately, my girl, you are even more so."

"Okay," she said, "give it to me straight. Are we talking family honor or the integrity of PAX here?"

"PAX."

"That's what I thought. You realize the photo pre-dates our agreement, don't you?"

"The photo, it seems, is the least of it now."

She took the skillet off the stove and ladled the mixture into two large serving dishes. "I thought you'd be furious to see me on the front page."

He filched a cookie from the jar near the refrigerator. The sight of her elegant uncle munching on a chocolate chip was amusing, but not amusing enough to divert her from the issue at hand. "An hour ago I was," he said, dusting his hands off on a square of paper towel. "Now there are more pressing problems."

"Have they called off the Summit?"

"The contrary. I wired the blueprints of The White Elephant to the home office last night."

"You FAXed them? Where on earth did you find a FAX machine at that hour?"

"Let us simply say that the accoutrements in a Rolls-Royce are second to none."

Maggie thought about her own dilapidated Jeep Cherokee and sighed. These days new windshield wiper blades were a luxury of the first order. "There are times I wonder why I ever left the organization."

"You fell in love," Alistair said, meeting her eyes. "Isn't that why?"

The reason, of course, had been much more complex than that. For her, love and loyalty had been inextricably bound, and when Rick Douglass said he needed her, she had turned her back on everything else.

"Why don't we cut to the issue at hand?" she said finally. "Do we have a security problem? Do we have too few bathrooms? Too many doors?" She forced a smile.

"Don't tell me the president requested a heart-shaped mattress."

For an answer, Alistair picked up a handful of fake twenties left behind by John Adams Tyler.

"Counterfeit money is a problem?" Maggie's laughter was genuine this time. "Really, Alistair, sometimes even PAX can go off the deep end."

Alistair's face seemed to register one conflicting emotion after another.

"What is it?" she prompted, pulling the hamburger rolls from the oven. "Angie will be in here any second."

"It's a delicate topic, Maggie, one that I hesitate to broach."

"Oh, for God's sake, Alistair! Since when have you stood on ceremony?"

To her utter amazement, Alistair's tanned cheeks turned bright pink, and he cleared his throat. "I must warn you about becoming involved during the time before the Summit."

"I don't know whether to laugh or hit you with a spatula! The only person I'm involved with is Colleen at the bank. She gives me advance warning when a check is going to bounce."

"That's not the type of involvement to which I refer, Maggie."

"That's what I was afraid of." She arranged the rolls in two wicker baskets and covered them with linen towels. "I'm not involved with anyone, Alistair." Indeed she hadn't been physically intimate with any man since losing Rick. Interested, yes, but the need was outweighed by the risks.

"That may not be the case for long."

She leaned against the counter and stared at her uncle. "I've heard about being the last to know, but this is carrying the concept a bit far. Do you mind telling me what you're talking about?''

"I'm talking about Mr. Tyler."

Damn it! Why did the mere mention of his name send currents of excitement zapping through her limbs?

Suddenly she was fifteen again and begging her best friend to recount a chance meeting at the water fountain. *Tell me everything. Is it the way he looks at me? Did he say something to his friends? Do you think he'll ask me to the prom?*

"What makes you think we'll become involved?" She wanted every juicy detail.

"I watched you two on the back porch."

"Oh." The kiss. "That's incredibly rude, Alistair."

"And the porch is incredibly public," he shot back. "You're moving rather quickly, are you not?"

"We're not moving at all." Angie had made certain to barge in on Maggie and John. Where was she now when Maggie needed her? "That was a social kiss. Nothing more."

She had no trouble translating Alistair's curse; this time it was pure Anglo-Saxon. "Don't take me for a fool, Magdalena."

"And don't take me for a liar, Alistair. I only met Tyler twenty-four hours ago and, if you'll recall, it was hardly under the most romantic of circumstances."

"Obviously things have changed."

"Obviously you're becoming paranoid. I saved his life. He wants to thank me. End of story." Forget the fact that the air between them had been charged with something that went far beyond simple gratitude.

"How quickly you've forgotten," Alistair said, lighting a Gauloise. "Paranoia is central to my profession."

"One of the many reasons I was glad to get out."

"Be that as it may, the payoff for you, if the Summit comes off as scheduled, is great. All I ask in return is for you to abide by a few simple guidelines." His cheeks grew taut as he inhaled on his cigarette, then they expanded as white smoke encircled his face. "I hardly think that is too much to ask."

"Tyler is a businessman, Alistair. Nothing more." The look she gave her uncle was sharper than the knife on the countertop. "Don't tell me you think that whole incident at the Bronze Penguin was a setup." She shook her head in disgust. "The man almost died! That's carrying paranoia above and beyond."

"Your naïveté is most unbecoming. How many times did we see the other side sacrifice operatives to a larger cause?"

The question was rhetorical. In truth Maggie couldn't begin to calculate the number of losses she'd heard about during her time with PAX.

"He's been on the cover of *Forbes* and *Newsweek*."

"All true," said Alistair. "He's also shared the spotlight in *Time* with Maximilian Steel."

"There! You see? That should prove he's legitimate." Maximilian Steel was the jet-propelled businessman who'd burst onto the scene a few years ago and ousted Donald Trump from his position as financial golden boy.

Alistair, however, remained unconvinced. "My girl, Steel is one of ours."

She had to hand it to him: he was really pulling out all the stops this time. "That's like telling me Warren Beatty is celibate. Steel is richer than all of the Rockefellers combined. Why in hell would he be mixed up with PAX?"

"Because, dear girl, nothing is ever as it seems. I would think, if you remember nothing from the old days, you would remember that." He watched her intently as she fumbled for her composure. "Steel is really a down-on-his-luck flight instructor who's a friend of Ryder O'Neal."

"But Steel has been in the papers for a few years now." Huge oil deals in Venezuela. Land in Brazil. Massive skyscrapers throughout Manhattan that put his rival, Trump, to shame. Steel had movie-star good looks, and the tabloids had been having a field day with him since the first day he appeared on the scene.

"Impressive, isn't it?" Alistair asked. "The setup has truly been a thing of beauty."

"Which brings me to the sixty-four-thousand-dollar question: Why are you telling me all of this?" It wasn't like Alistair to speak of sensitive topics this freely.

"I'm telling you because you must understand that in this world anything is possible. Mr. Tyler may be exactly as he appears." He took a long drag on his cigarette. "And then again, he may not."

A shiver snaked its way up her spine, and she did her best to dismiss it as the result of too much air-conditioning against the heavy August heat.

She pointed toward the boxes of fake money by the door. "I'm having dinner with him tonight," she said, aware she sounded more like a rebellious child than a woman of almost thirty-five. "If I don't, there's no telling what stunt he'll pull next."

"Have your dinner," said Alistair. "The last thing I want is for him to grow suspicious."

The first gorgeous single man she'd seen in ages, and her uncle had to think he was a communist spy. Rachel was right: There was no justice in the world.

"You don't *really* think he's in on something, do you?"

His shrug was eloquent. "Of course, I'll be running the usual check on him. We'll know soon enough, won't we, dear girl?"

Not terribly encouraging.

However, she couldn't follow up on that statement because Angie chose that moment to burst into the room.

"Horseback riding makes them ravenous!" Angie quickly piled the dishes and bowls and baskets on a huge metal try. "You'd think *they* were the ones who did all the work."

Maggie saw Alistair out to the Rolls parked in her rutted driveway.

"Take care," he said. "Remember there may be more to Mr. Tyler than meets the eye." He leaned over and kissed her cheek. "That is from Holland. We're leaving as soon as I get back to the cottage."

Maggie raised up on her toes and kissed his weathered cheek lightly in return. As always, he smelled vaguely of cinnamon and spice and, despite herself, she smiled. "That's for Holland. Give her my love."

He chucked her lightly under the chin the way he used to do when she was a child. "No fond goodbye for your aged uncle?"

"You're lucky I don't give you a flat tire." She gave the Rolls a gentle kick with the toe of her right Reebok. "Now I'll be seeing trouble around every corner between now and the Summit Meeting."

"Good," said her uncle. "We can't afford to be too careful."

She watched him roar off down the lane that led to the main road, the silver Rolls-Royce a reminder of the world of privilege and danger that existed beyond the confines of sleepy East Point.

From now until mid-September, PAX would be hiding behind the bushes and lurking under the drainpipes. There would be transmitters in the vases and microphones behind the potted palms in her Victorian dining room.

And now that John Adams Tyler was under suspicion, there would probably even be a camera or two neatly tucked behind those infamous mirrored ceilings, eliminating a few of the more exotic fantasies Maggie had entertained last night.

But what did it matter? John Adams Tyler wasn't even her type.

Three-piece suits and silk ties and impeccable business credentials were commonplace in the world she'd once inhabited. Tyler was stamped out of the same WASPy, Wonder Bread mold of nearly every man she'd met when she worked for PAX.

He was every bit as—

She stopped dead on the top step. No, it was just too ridiculous to even consider.

John Adams Tyler couldn't be a spy.

Or could he?

MAGGIE SCOOPED UP her car keys from the end table near the reservations desk.

"I'm off," she said to Rachel, who'd come over to help with the dinner rush.

Rachel glanced at her watch. "Fashionably late. Aren't you afraid the gorgeous Mr. Tyler will be offended?"

"I'm a working woman, Rae. He'll just have to understand the burdens we peons carry." She pirouetted, the skirt of her buttercup-yellow dress swirling about her knees. "How do I look?"

"The dress looks marvelous," Rachel said, "and you know I'd kill to have your legs." She leaned back against the rolltop desk and shook her head. "But there's something wrong."

"I don't have time to change," Maggie warned her mother-in-law, "so don't bother suggesting that I slip into something slinky and black."

Rachel's hand flew to her throat in feigned surprise. "I wouldn't think of it, honey. There's something to be said for the Sister Mary Francis look."

"Very funny." While her silky knit dress wasn't exactly straight from the Fredericks of Hollywood summer catalog, it wasn't convent material, either. She grabbed Rachel's wrist and checked the time herself. "You have exactly ten seconds to voice your complaints, then I'm out of here."

"I only need two. It's your attitude."

"My attitude?"

"Your attitude. You're going off to Hideaway Haven to have a romantic dinner with the gorgeous, single, *rich* owner of the place, and you look like you're going to Dr. Jay for a root canal. What gives?"

"Nothing." *Oh, Rachel, do I have a story for you!* "This is strictly business."

"No, honey. Lunch at the Bronze Penguin is strictly business. This is definitely extracurricular."

"Here!" She flipped her mother-in-law her car keys. "If you're so interested, why don't you go?"

Rachel laughed and handed them back to Maggie. "Because I'd hate to see the look on Mr. Tyler's face when I knocked on the front door. It's you he wants, honey. Let's not disappoint him."

DISAPPOINTING John Adams Tyler was the last thing on Maggie's mind as she drove through the ivy-covered gates and entered the world of Hideaway Haven.

She was more concerned with keeping her car on the road.

Bowers of roses, entwined on huge trellises, framed the roadway, which was beautifully lighted by old-fashioned gas lamps.

Road signs coyly painted with lovers strolling hand in hand warned drivers to watch out for Dear Crossing. To her right, a tiny covered bridge spanned a small stream. Kissing Bridge, said the sign, reviving an old Pennsylvania custom.

The old Pennsylvanians would be *very* surprised.

The Kissing Bridge was followed quickly by the Kissing Flower Garden and the Kissing Roller Rink, and as Maggie guided her car up the hill she wouldn't have been the least surprised if the Kissing Bathroom was right around the bend.

She stopped near a pitch 'n' putt golf course while three laughing couples rode past on bicycles built for two. Two of the couples were obviously yuppies who, in the outside world, wouldn't be caught dead without their BMWs, while the other couple wore matching Mohawks and silver earrings and probably struck terror into the hearts of their neighbors back home.

To Maggie's intense surprise, they didn't seem the least embarrassed by their surroundings. In fact, they seemed to be having a terrific time.

Could it be something in the air around there? A special chemical Tyler mixed in with the bug spray that lowered a person's resistance to bad taste? Cautiously she lowered her window a crack and breathed the rose-scented air. It seemed normal enough, but then you could never tell about things like that until it was too late.

If this was a cover for some devious plot, then it was the most ingenious one she'd ever seen.

Alistair had to be wrong. No self-respecting operative would be caught dead in the middle of such all-American kitsch.

Well, maybe that *was* a poor choice of words, but it was hard to imagine dour Eastern-bloc socialist types reveling among the roses and canoeing on the lake.

Even at night—and despite the tacky trappings—she could see that the grounds of Hideaway Haven were extraordinary. Huge expanses of green lawn spread across the countryside like a mantle, dotted here and there with wildflowers that even an expert gardener couldn't tame. The buildings she passed were all freshly painted. Unlike the shutters at The White Elephant, the shutters at Hideaway Haven proudly flanked windows that most likely sparkled like diamonds in the sunlight.

The buildings were perfect.

The grounds were perfect.

The owner was perfect.

She thought of her hand-to-mouth operation at The White Elephant.

It was all too depressing for words.

Maggie pulled into the guest parking lot and settled her car into a spot nestled between a BMW and a '66 Corvette. A beat-up Jeep was parked three spots down, and a Ford Escort that had seen better days was near the door.

Apparently the appeal of the place transcended socioeconomic barriers. It was getting tougher to maintain her preconceptions about Hideaway Haven.

She took her time strolling up to the main house, stopping to sniff the clouds of roses and marigolds and zinnias marking the path to the front door.

At least he hadn't sacrificed real flowers for fake. Spy or not, there was still hope for him.

The door swung open before she had a chance to knock.

Decked out in a gray silk suit and ruby tie stood John Adams Tyler.

"Come in," he said, opening the door wide and ushering her inside. "Welcome to Hideaway Haven."

*Said the spider to the fly.*

# Chapter Eight

"Did you say something?" John asked as he closed the door behind her.

She made her eyes wide and innocent. "Did you hear something?"

"I thought so."

"Hello." She smiled sweetly. "For the second time."

"So, you *did* say something."

"Of course I did. A good guest always says hello when her host opens the door."

His eyes blazed with intelligence and humor, and she knew he didn't believe one damned word she was saying.

Score one for Mr. Tyler.

"I'll find out, sooner or later," he said as he led her into the huge foyer that served as lobby for the main building.

"Don't be so sure." She ran her finger over the highly polished surface of an antique mahogany desk she would sell her soul for. "I won't be here long enough."

"Don't be so sure," he countered. His fingers were lightly possessive at the small of her back as he guided her through a hallway lined with oil portraits of eighteenth- and nineteenth-century men and women who all looked vaguely like Tyler himself. "You may be here longer than you think."

A voluptuous shiver began at the point where his fingers rested and rippled throughout her body. It would almost be easier to deal with him if he was a spy. She knew how to handle spies.

Men, even if they weren't her type, were another matter entirely.

She searched around quickly for another, less volatile topic of conversation.

"I apologize for being late," she said as he led her into a glass-enclosed room overlooking the lake. "We ran out of prime ribs, and I had to send Rachel over to—" She glanced up at him, a smile tugging at the right-hand corner of her mouth. "Aren't you going to stop me?"

"I hadn't planned on it." He motioned her to the love seat facing the window, then crossed to the bar in the far corner. "Mumm's Cordon Rouge or Taittinger?"

"What?"

"Champagne." He held up two unopened bottles. "Mumm's or Taittinger."

She thought of the bottle of Gallo Chablis sitting alone in her refrigerator. "Your choice." With due respect to Ernest and Julio, she doubted she could lose.

"Taittinger," he said, putting the other bottle away and reaching for the cork puller. "You sent Rachel out to do what?"

Her mind was devoid of all but delicious anticipation as she watched him open the bottle of champagne.

"Why you were late," he prompted. "You ran out of prime ribs, and you sent someone named Rachel over to—"

Good memory.

Bad sign.

Operatives usually had superlative memories.

"You really don't want to hear the gory details, do you?"

"Sure." He handed her a fluted crystal glass of champagne. "Good business. It never hurts to hear about the competition's problems."

She made a show of inspecting the Chippendale side table to her right, the private lake beyond the French doors, the golden bubbly in her glass. "Why is it I feel you just don't have my kind of problems?"

"We all have the same problems," he said, sitting at the other end of the sofa. "It's only a matter of degree."

"Ah, yes. Perspective, isn't it?"

His smile told her he was pleased she remembered his words from that afternoon. She wondered if she'd made a tactical mistake, but the view was too alluring, and the champagne too wonderful to worry much about it.

She would just have to make a point to be more careful.

He lifted his glass toward her. "To dramatic rescues. I owe you."

She touched her glass to his, then took a long, luscious sip of champagne, sighing with pleasure as the bubbles tickled their way down her throat. "Consider the debt repaid. This is marvelous!"

"Only the best." His eyes met hers.

"Is that one of your rules for success in business?"

"For success in everything."

His gaze never wavered. An unnerving sensation of warmth spread outward from her chest. Back in her days with PAX, she would have known how to turn a moment like this around to her advantage, to seize the emotional energy and defuse a situation that grew more volatile, more dangerous with every second.

But she wasn't with PAX any longer. She was a woman who owned a run-down honeymoon hotel in the middle of nowhere. A woman who wore jeans and denim shirts more often than not.

A woman who had forgotten that the nearness of a man could be more intoxicating than even champagne.

"More?"

"I haven't finished—" She looked at her empty glass and shrugged. "Well, maybe I will. Thanks."

He leaned over to pluck the bottle from the stand next to him. His suit jacket was unbuttoned, and as he reached, his shirt strained across his muscular chest.

It didn't take a great leap of imagination to recall exactly how muscular that particular chest was, or how the whorl of dark curls felt against her cheek, or how warm and resilient his skin had seemed against her lips....

What she wanted to do was reach into the ice bucket, grab a cube and place it against her pulse points before she went up in flames.

What she did was hold out her glass for a refill and take another sip.

"She went to Kenny's Steak & Ale and bought up all their prime ribs."

"She did what?"

So that was how to break his concentration.

Maggie waved her hand impatiently in the air. "Rachel. She went to Kenny's and bought up the prime ribs." She waited. He still looked confused. "For dinner at The White Elephant. Remember? You were going to learn from my mistakes."

"Who is Rachel?"

Maggie polished off her second glass of champagne. "My mother-in-law."

Despite the friendly champagne haze cushioning her brain, Maggie knew a pregnant pause when she heard one.

"You're married." It was a statement, not a question. "Maybe we should have dinner."

"I *was* married," Maggie corrected him, wishing he'd offer her a third glass of champagne. "Rick died four years ago."

"Accident?"

"No." She extended her empty glass. "I'd love a little more."

He emptied the rest of the bottle into her glass, but it wasn't nearly enough to deaden the sudden stab of pain.

Tyler was watching her. Those golden eyes seemed to zero right in on her weak spots.

"Rick died of cancer." Her voice was low and controlled. "He shouldn't have, but he did all the same. It was slow, ugly and painful, and when it finally happened it was almost a relief." Damn the champagne. She'd said more to this stranger than she had to her own uncle on the topic.

Tyler walked over to the bar, poured himself a whiskey and downed it in one gulp.

"Serves you right," she said, resting her empty glass on the Chippendale. "You shouldn't have asked."

He leaned against the bar, palms down, arms extended. "I had to ask."

That same intense energy she'd experienced the moment he entered the Bronze Penguin—was it only yesterday?—resurfaced and caused her to throw discretion to the four winds. "You had to ask if I was married?"

"Yep. No choice involved."

"It makes a difference?"

He nodded, his face unreadable. "A big difference."

"Married women can't save your life?"

"That's not what I meant."

She didn't think so, not really. "I think it's time for dinner."

He stepped out from behind the bar and walked toward her, his big body loose limbed and athletic beneath the dismaying confines of his suit. He had no business wearing a suit like that. Suits were for men like her Uncle Alistair who rode around in silver Rolls-Royces and dined in places like Le Cirque and Lutece.

Tyler should be wearing faded jeans that dipped low over his navel and a cotton work shirt open to the waist.

If he had any decency at all, he would turn himself into the kind of man she fantasized about—a ridiculous dream.

He was a dyed-in-the-wool executive type whose diapers had probably been lined with *The Wall Street Journal* and whose first word had been "dividend."

"Stand up," he said as he stopped in front of her.

"Get lost," she said mildly.

He extended his hand. "Stand up," he repeated.

"I don't take orders."

He started to laugh. "You can't stand up, can you?"

"Of course I can." She started to rise, but the effort made her head spin. "At least I thought I could." She sat back down and rested her head against the arm of the couch. "I don't believe this! Thirty-four years old and I can't handle two lousy glasses of champagne."

"Three glasses," he said, "not that we're counting. And that's the first time I've heard anyone call Taittinger 'lousy.'"

The room tilted at an alarming angle, and she closed her eyes. "Don't be difficult. I'm feeling too awful to be made fun of."

"No one's making fun of you, Maggie." His voice came at her from at least three different directions. Maybe she was being held captive by the Andrews Sisters on steroids. "Have you eaten yet?"

She opened her eyes and tried to remember, but her mind was like overstretched Turkish taffy. "Did you serve dinner yet?"

"Not yet."

She closed her eyes again. "Then I haven't eaten."

"What about lunch?"

"I don't know. But I know about breakfast. I hate it. Runny eggs, raw bacon, burned toast—" She shivered. "Awful meal."

"You mean you didn't eat at all today?"

Her bare shoulders slid down against the silky couch cover and she shrugged. "Guess not," she managed. "Who has time?"

"Three glasses of champagne on an empty stomach. I'm surprised you know your own name."

She drooped even lower as his large hands closed around her ankles, and he put her feet up on the couch.

"Are you going to take advantage of me?" she asked, opening one eye. Spies often did things like that.

"Not this time."

"I'm too inebriated to defend myself."

"I know," he said. "That's why."

"I thought you would kiss me again."

"Oh, I'm going to kiss you again, Maggie Douglass, but when I do, I want you to know about it."

"In the interest of fairness," she said, her voice slurring the words together in a champagne fog, "I should tell you you're not my type."

"Oh, yeah?" He sounded amused. Normally that would have enraged her, but she was simply too tired to care. "Take a nap, and we'll talk about that later."

"Dinner," she said, already drifting away into sleep. "You promised me dinner..."

"Sleep, Maggie. You're going to need it."

"What do you mean by that?"

"You'll find out soon enough."

For one brief lucid moment, Maggie knew that if she didn't get up off that couch and get back home, her life would never be the same again.

She should get up and search for secret documents and phone scramblers and sophisticated transmitters so powerful they could pick up her heartbeat.

She should at the very least sit up and stay awake.

The man was obviously a dangerous spy set on using his sex appeal to torture PAX's secrets out of her poor champagne-soaked brain.

All in all, it didn't sound half-bad.

She was asleep before he left the room.

JOHN WALKED through the hallway, elbowed his way past a cluster of newlyweds in the lobby, then flung open the front door.

The evening air was still heavy with the day's heat, but he didn't notice it.

He tore around to the side of the main house, grabbed the hose Raymond used to water the herb gardens, then turned it full force on himself.

Icy water dripped down his face and onto his expensive suit.

He didn't give a damn.

He deserved the Congressional Medal of Honor, the Croix de Guerre and the Purple Heart for what he did back there in the sun room.

For what he *didn't* do.

What red-blooded, heterosexual American male would have turned away from Maggie Douglass?

A liberated jerk, that's who.

Even now, with the cold water doing its damnedest to bring his overheated libido back within range, he couldn't help wondering if another man would have ignored the delicacy of the situation and turned too much champagne into something more interesting.

Hell.

Ten or fifteen years ago, John would have been one of them.

If a woman like Maggie Douglass had appeared before him, vulnerable and beautiful, he wouldn't have hesitated longer than it took to whisper the words "trust me" in the curve of her ear.

He'd left the Mr. Nice Guy image behind, right along with the dreams he'd lost when Laura married another man.

Okay, so maybe he'd been a slow learner, maybe he'd taken a hell of a lot longer than normal to learn that life didn't always provide a happy ending for those who wait. Maybe for a while there he had taken a walk on the wild side.

And discovered he wasn't the type.

You couldn't be descended from John and Abigail, the original American romantics, and be anything but marriage material. It was in his blood and in his bones and, sexual revolution or no sexual revolution, he wanted the happily-ever-after as much as any 1950s heroine.

So he'd waited and he'd looked and, on occasion, he'd sampled, but he hadn't found the other half of his heart.

Until Maggie Douglass.

He thought about how she looked, stretched out on his silk-covered couch, her long hair drifting across her shoulders and breasts like a mantle of fiery gold. She had the face of an angel and the body of—hell, the kind of body men dream about.

She also had wit and intelligence and ambition, and everything else wonderful in a woman.

This was Kismet.

This was destiny.

This was every sappy line from "Some Enchanted Evening" come to life right there in East Point.

By the end of next month there'd be a wedding, or he'd know the reason why.

# Chapter Nine

"I should be humiliated," Maggie said for the tenth time as she polished off the rest of her raspberry soufflé. "If I weren't so hungry, I would be."

Across the table, John poured them each more coffee. "There's some cheesecake in the refrigerator if you're interested."

Maggie groaned and pushed her chair away from the table. "I'm interested," she said, trying valiantly to ignore the untouched piece of chocolate pie on John's plate, "but I shouldn't add gluttony to my list of transgressions."

"The food meets with your approval?"

She tried to smother a smile but failed miserably. "It's not sloppy joes, but you can't have everything."

"We try," he said, pushing his chocolate pie toward her. "We try."

As much as she hated to admit it, the food at Hideaway Haven was superb.

*Oh, go all the way, Douglass,* she thought, glancing at the miniature roses in the centerpiece, the candles twinkling from silver sconces on the wall, the lustrous Oriental carpet underfoot.

Everything about Hideaway Haven was first-rate.

She glanced at John, then looked away.

Including her dinner companion, a man who bore little resemblance to the cool, worldly businessman who'd greeted her at the door.

Magically the multimillionaire owner of half the Poconos had disappeared while she shamelessly slept on his couch and, in his place, was a somewhat rumpled, and dangerously sexy man.

She'd enjoyed a deep and wonderful sleep. Who wouldn't have with the French doors open onto the lake, the soft evening breezes feathering across her and the moon rising silver over the pine trees?

She awoke after a time to find him standing near those doors, watching her. He no longer wore the suit; instead he had changed into a pair of dark pants and a cotton fisherman's sweater. His hair looked as if it had been freshly washed. Where it grew down over his collar in the back, the strands were dark and wet.

Her resolve slipped another notch at that moment, and she had thanked the patron saint of weak-willed women that at Hideaway Haven they served dinner on demand.

"Are you sure you don't want a little cheesecake?" John asked as she sipped her after-dinner coffee.

"You're tempting me."

"That's the general idea."

"No," she said, conjuring up visions of PAX and hidden microphones and her glowering uncle. "I'm good at resisting temptation."

"I'm not," he said, his golden eyes glittering in the candlelight. "Put temptation in my path, and I'll give in every time."

"I'm made of sterner stuff," she said, not at all certain she could fool him. "Denial is good for the soul."

"We could debate that issue."

"I'd rather not. Temptation is like politics and religion—not dinnertime conversation." She raised her coffee cup to her lips.

"Sex," said John.

The coffee missed her mouth and dribbled down her chin. "I beg your pardon?" She reached for her napkin and blotted her face before the spill reached the snowy tablecloth. Had he been talking to her parrot, Groucho?

"Sex," said Tyler, not missing a beat. "It's sex, politics and religion."

"I was paraphrasing."

"You were equivocating."

"If you'll recall, I was talking about cheesecake, not a weekend in the country with Warren Beatty."

"I wouldn't mind talking about a weekend in the country."

She arched her brows. "With Warren Beatty?"

"With you."

"I'm sure you wouldn't," she said smoothly, despite the sudden acceleration of her heart. "You own most of the countryside around here."

"So we're back to business again?"

"Why not? You said yourself that we should learn from our competition."

"Sometimes I talk too much." He polished off the rest of his coffee, then stood up. "Let's get the guided tour out of the way."

"Be still, my heart!" She feigned a swoon. "The inside of the pleasure palace. I'll never be the same again."

"If you're lucky, you won't be." He extended his hand to her.

"Aren't you worried I might steal the secrets of your success?" Her hand disappeared within his. It felt better than it should, which was probably a bad sign, but at the moment she was too full and too content to be concerned with spies and counterspies.

"Not at all."

"No skeletons in your closet."

"No skeletons."

He looked as if he were telling the truth, and Maggie had to remind herself that at PAX everyone looked as if they were telling the truth, even when they were concocting the most outrageous lies.

"I warn you I'm incredibly nosy," she said as they left the private dining room. "Nothing escapes my notice."

"I'll keep that in mind." His grip on her hand grew stronger while her reserve grew weaker.

She'd already discovered that the lobby was indeed a rosy pink from ceiling to carpet, so the second time around it didn't faze her quite as much. He led her up a winding open staircase.

"Sexist," she muttered. "If anyone were sitting down there I could be arrested for indecent exposure."

"I wouldn't press charges."

"How kind of you."

"Now I see why you do such lousy business."

She pulled her hand from his and stopped on the second-floor landing. "Been spying again, Mr. Tyler?"

He didn't even blink. "Didn't have to. It's your attitude I'm talking about."

She laughed out loud. "That and the million dollars I don't have."

"You just don't understand the rationale behind the Poconos, do you?"

"Oh, great!" She followed him up another flight of stairs. "Philosophy from a man whose idea of culture is a vibrating water bed."

"You ever tried one?"

"I've led a sheltered life."

"Too bad. If you'd put your elitist attitude on hold for a while, you might find you like it."

"I'm opting for class."

"You're opting for bankruptcy."

He took her hand again and propelled her down the length of the third-floor hallway. The pink plush carpet was so thick she felt as if she were running in quicksand.

She wished she could kick off her heels and sink barefoot into that decadent luxury; however, a move like that would be a dead giveaway, and she didn't want to give Tyler the satisfaction.

He stopped in front of a pair of double oak doors at the end of the hallway and inserted a key in the lock on the right-hand side.

The words, Garden of Eden, were emblazoned across the top rail in shiny brass letters, and she was wondering how many people he had on staff to polish the nameplates on two hundred and fifty rooms just like this one when he flung the door open and unceremoniously yanked her inside.

"Just what do you think you're—" Her protest died on her lips as she took in her surroundings. "I don't *believe* this," she whispered. In her wildest dreams, she could never have imagined anything like it.

In his wildest dreams, Hugh Hefner couldn't have imagined anything like it.

"What do you think?" Tyler's chest was puffed out with the pride of a new father showing off his infant son. "This was the prototype for the Love Cottages."

Maggie gawked at her surroundings. "I'm in shock," she managed finally. "I'm beyond conscious thought."

Oh, she'd seen Margo Wayne's Pocono Playpen and Ed Gianelli's Roman tubs with their super bubble bath, but she'd never seen anything like this.

John Adams Tyler did things on a grand scale, even in prototype. Mirrors of smoked glass reached from the plushly carpeted floor to the cathedral ceiling, reflecting the lush, throbbing pinks, reds and purples of the decor.

The windows were draped in heavy folds of purple velvet that matched the curtains draping the bed. Closed, the effect would be almost womblike, a deep comforting effortless sensation of sensuality and privacy.

From the massive round water bed to the Jacuzzi, everything in the three-room suite had been created with one purpose, and one purpose only, in mind.

"This is a candy store for adults," she said finally. "A sexual Disneyland."

"I knew you'd like it."

She shot him a look that was reflected back at her in the wall of smoked glass mirrors. "I never said I liked it. This place is crass and vulgar and—"

"Booked solid. You can't fight success, Maggie. Give the public what it wants, and they'll build a highway to your door."

"It looks like a hot sheet motel, Tyler. Five dollars for five hours."

He picked up a champagne glass from the marble bar near the fireplace. "You don't find Waterford crystal in a hot sheet motel."

"Big deal," she countered, mesmerized by the way the water bed moved with a Jello-like life of its own. "I still don't like it."

"That's why you're going out of business, Maggie Douglass."

"The hell I am, Tyler. I'm in the process of revitalizing The White Elephant."

"You're in the process of hanging on by your polished fingernails."

"And I suppose mirrored ceilings are the answer to my prayers?"

"Could be." Damn him. Those golden eyes of his twinkled more brightly than a hundred candles. "They're sure as hell the answer to mine."

God knew she didn't want to smile at the lout, but the urge was getting the better of her. "Why is it I have the feeling you're not talking about your fiscal health anymore?"

He touched a button on a console near the bar, and music, soft and low and dangerously romantic, filled the room.

"Because you're as bright as you are beautiful, Maggie." His arms went around her, and he drew her close. "Because you know something's happening between us."

"Because I'm losing my mind." Her head found the perfect resting spot on his broad shoulder as they began to sway gently to the music.

"Admit it's getting to you." His breath was warm against her ear. "The music, the lights, the scent of roses in the air."

It was getting to her, all right. Her mind was turning into cotton candy, and this time she couldn't blame champagne. "It's tacky," she managed, her voice low and husky.

"Sure, it's tacky. But it works."

The music grew slower, and their movements slowed until they were embracing more than dancing.

"Honeymoons are all about sex, Maggie," he said softly. "That's the reason for it all."

Her heart labored inside her chest, and she doubted she could draw a deep breath.

"Honeymoons are a vacation," she said. "Like a trip to Bermuda."

"This isn't Bermuda. We don't have beaches made of pink sand or bobbies in white shorts and high hats or fancy boutiques. We're offering a different kind of fantasy."

She said nothing. She didn't trust her voice.

"You were married," he persisted. "You had a honeymoon."

"Hawaii," she managed. "Seven days."

"Was it wonderful?"

She shrugged in his arms. "Awkward at best," she said honestly. "Rick got sunstroke. I was stung by a bee. We spent a lot of time in our room watching television." She'd gone to her marriage bed, sophisticated in the ways of the world but painfully innocent and awkward when it came to the realities of love.

Those seven days in that tiny hotel room had been an agony of embarrassment.

"Honeymoons are overrated," she said. "We put too much emphasis on performance."

"But newlyweds are still going to take them," John said. "It's a rite of passage. That's why places like this are so important."

"And I suppose you're East Point's answer to Mother Theresa."

"I give them what they need, Maggie. Luxury they'll never have again in their lifetime. A huge water bed to play in, a massive Jacuzzi to relax in, fireplaces and champagne and mirrored ceilings—"

"You're describing a bordello, Tyler."

"Exactly. A bordello for monogamous newlyweds. What's wrong with that?"

"I'm starting to think you're crazy."

"And I'm starting to think you're not as smart as you look. Think back, Maggie. You're young, you're just married, all the pressures of adulthood are swooping down on you quicker than you can say mister and missus. In nine months you might even have your first child. Where better to make the transition than in a place like this that's so absurd and so blatantly sexy you can't help laughing about it?" He tilted her head back so she was forced to meet his eyes.

"You're the strangest man I've ever met, John Adams Tyler." And with her background in PAX, that was saying something. "And this is definitely the strangest place."

"I think you like it here."

She ducked her head so he wouldn't see her smile. "I think you're crazy."

"Admit it. Red plush wallpaper turns you on."

She stole a glance at the mirrors surrounding the water bed. "I don't care what you say, I just can't imagine my Uncle Alistair cavorting under a smoked glass mirror."

"You'd be surprised. We had a couple here last month to celebrate their golden anniversary."

"Not in a room like this!"

"Why not in a room like this?" He was smooth, John Tyler was. He probably thought she didn't realize he was dancing her closer to the bed.

"It's—how can I put it? Unseemly."

"Well, the room wasn't exactly like this."

Her smile was wide with relief. "I'm so glad to hear that."

"Actually there was a hammock suspended near the Jacuzzi and a giant swing that—"

"You're joking," she said. "Tell me you're joking."

"I'm serious. I can show you the guest register if you like."

"Whatever happened to growing old gracefully?"

"Whatever happened to enjoying life?"

How would she know?

Most of her marriage had been spent watching her husband die. A lusty celebration of life between man and woman was something she'd never experienced.

And certainly not in a hammock next to a Jacuzzi shaped like a champagne glass, bubbles and all.

"It's late," she said, at last. "I should be getting back."

"It's not even midnight yet."

"I'm understaffed, remember? Breakfast comes early in the Poconos."

"Your guests come down for breakfast?"

She nodded. "Naturally."

"You definitely have a lot to learn, Maggie. Add a water bed and a few mirrors to those cottages of yours, and you won't see a newlywed before lunchtime."

She started to say that that was the first good reason she'd heard for tacky decor, when a quick series of five beeps sounded.

"Is that a fire alarm?" She looked quickly around the suite for smoke.

"Nothing that exciting. It's the front desk." He pulled a beeper from his back pocket. "I'll be right back."

Apparently phones next to the bed weren't appreciated in fantasyland, and Tyler disappeared into another part of the suite where such mundane activities as telephoning were carried out.

The second he disappeared around the corner, Maggie did a quick, but thorough check for bugs or hidden cameras.

Nothing.

Of course, that didn't really mean a thing. If Tyler was an operative, he wouldn't be careless enough to leave her in a room with an easy-to-uncover bug.

Besides, it was almost impossible to keep her mind on nonsense like spies and super summit meetings when she was standing in a room designed for nothing more than sensual pleasures of the ultimate kind.

She ran her hand over the flocked red wallpaper, laughing softly as it tickled her palm. Mae West would have been in her glory in a place like this. Chandeliers dripped crystal beads the way Liz Taylor dripped diamonds. Fur throw rugs framed the fireplace. The champagne-glass Jacuzzi bubbled invitingly on the upper level balcony overlooking the sitting area.

"Sitting area," she mumbled, watching herself reflected in mirror after mirror after mirror. There was a euphemism for you.

She doubted if many of the Love Cottage couples did much sitting. Not with that huge water bed undulating under its purple satin spread.

How on earth did couples make love while the bed sloshed around them like the Delaware River in a storm?

A ridiculous vision of a new bride approaching her new husband dressed in a filmy negligee and life preserver made her laugh out loud.

When newlyweds at Hideaway Haven talked about The Pill, they probably meant Dramamine.

She glanced toward the other end of the suite. Tyler's voice, low and authoritative, bounced off the indoor pool and back at her.

"...plumber...insurance agent can...damn it, put her on the phone..."

He sounded as if he'd be busy a while longer.

This was her chance.

Maggie kicked off her heels and approached the bed. She rested her hand on the mattress and shrugged.

Not so different from her Sealy Posturepedic.

Maybe this was another case of all hype and no substance.

She'd take her investigation further.

The mattress rested inside what appeared to be a huge wooden box that nipped at the back of her legs as she gingerly sat down.

Well, she meant to sit down, but the damned bed seemed to have other ideas.

The moment her fanny hit the spread, the bed leaped to life, as if high tide and low tide had met right there in the middle.

Physicists were right. For every action there *was* a reaction. As her bottom sank like the *Titanic*, her legs shot toward the mirrored ceiling, and her yellow skirt sailed up her thighs. She struggled to pull herself back to a sitting position, but she bobbed helplessly like a shipwrecked sailor looking for land.

It was bad enough she had to watch this pathetic scene reflected in the floor-to-ceiling mirrors that surrounded this monstrosity Tyler called a bed; the view in the mirrored ceiling was pathetic.

"...you tell them I said so," John's voice boomed from the other room. "I'll be there as soon as I can."

Maggie's eyes closed in despair.

*Please, God, just a small earthquake—a two or a three on the Richter scale.*

Just enough to swallow her up, bed and all, before Tyler discovered her lying like a huge yellow canary with a very red face.

Forget dignity.

She was talking survival!

# Chapter Ten

"Sorry I kept you waiting so long, Maggie. They wanted me to—"

He stopped dead in the doorway and stared at her, at the mirrors, then back at her again.

*All the better to see you with, my dear.*

The image was already burned into her brain. Hair tumbling all over the place, her wayward skirt inching up her thighs, her face flaming redder than the wallpaper.

"Stop staring at me!" she snapped. "This damned thing is alive!"

"Right," he said, approaching the edge of the bed. "It reached up and grabbed you."

"I sat down to adjust my shoe."

He looked over at the pale yellow pumps peeking out from under the chair across the room. "You can do better than that, Maggie."

"The least you could do is stop laughing, Tyler. You're making it very hard for me to retain my dignity."

"Forget your dignity," he said as she scrambled to her knees and tried to edge her way over to him. "You lost it when you fell asleep on the sofa." His smile widened maddeningly. "You snore, Maggie."

"I do not!"

"Afraid so."

"I was probably clearing my throat."

"For fifteen minutes straight?"

"I refuse to believe it."

"I'll tape it next time."

She lost her balance and fell back against the pillows in a flash of thigh and hip. "Read my lips, Tyler. There isn't going to be a next time."

"Sorry," he said, moving closer still. "It's beyond your control, Maggie."

"Nothing is beyond my control. If you don't help me up, I'll scream this place down."

He sat on the edge and extended his hand to her. "Use me for support and just slide over. It's not difficult once you get the hang of it."

She grabbed his hand and maneuvered her way toward him. "I feel like a jerk," she muttered, leaning against him and swinging her legs over the side. "First I snore on your couch, and now I can't get out of bed without assistance. Next you'll be feeding me strained bananas."

"I don't mind."

"I do. This will probably be an anecdote in tomorrow's *Pocono Bugle*."

"Only if you call it in."

Her right eyebrow arched. "Have no fear. This is one secret that will die with me."

"Terrific. A courtship should be private."

She moved away. "Courtship?"

"You know, courtship. Dinner and movies. Lots of kissing. Watching the sun set over the Delaware Water Gap. Considering your business, it shouldn't be an alien concept."

"You *are* crazy."

"Never saner."

"Maybe I didn't do such a great job of saving your life. I think the lack of oxygen did something to your brain."

"Trust me on this one, Maggie. I know exactly what I'm saying."

She felt as if someone had strapped her into the front seat of a roller coaster and forgotten to let her off.

"You've carried gratitude far enough, John." If her feet could only reach the ground, she'd stand up. "Help me up. I want to go home."

"Not until you hear me out."

"This is kidnapping."

"The hell it is." He drew her closer to him, and there was nothing she could do to hold him off. Sitting upright was enough to cope with at the moment. "You came here of your own free will."

"You're detaining me against my own free will. I'll bring you up on charges."

"Why bother? A wife can't testify against her husband."

"I'll call my lawyer and—" Maybe she was the one who was crazy. "What did you say?"

"This isn't the way I had it planned, Maggie."

"I'll give you ten seconds to explain yourself, Tyler."

"I'm going to marry you."

Her breath slid from her body in one sibilant whoosh. "You're serious."

"From the first second I saw you."

"Maybe you should see a psychiatrist."

He tangled his hand in her hair, and her entire body responded to his touch. "Why?" His voice was scuffed velvet. "Because I've fallen in love with you?"

"People don't fall in love at first sight."

He traced the curve of her ear with his thumb. She hadn't breathed normally since he sat down next to her.

"They do in my family. Two hundred and fifty years' worth of love at first sight."

"I'm impressed."

"I'm glad. I don't believe in long engagements."

"I said I'm impressed, John; I didn't say I do."

He pressed a kiss against her ear at the spot where his finger had rested. Her body trembled as desire, heated and wild, flooded through her.

"No sense fighting it." He kissed her ear, her cheekbone, the left corner of her mouth. "It's destiny."

"Your destiny." She struggled against the surge of emotion building inside her. "Not mine."

His lips were warm against her jaw. "I come from a family of romantics."

"I come from a family of realists," she managed, the ability to think deserting her as he kissed his way down her throat. "Things like this just don't happen in real life."

"Sure they do." He nipped gently at her collarbone. "They just never happened to you before."

He kissed his way back up toward her mouth, and she was overcome with desire to know the taste and feel of his lips and tongue.

"I should be afraid of you," she whispered as her hands splayed across the corded muscles of his shoulders. "If I had any sense at all, I'd run for my life."

He drew back, his golden eyes dark and commanding. "You can," he said. "If that's what you really want."

But of course she had no earthly idea what she wanted. How could she?

What was happening between them in that room had nothing to do with the world as she knew it, the world where she worked hard by day and slept alone each night.

It could have been Shangri-la or Xanadu or any other mythical, magical fantasy world where men were men and women were extremely happy.

"There's no future for us," she said, pushing a lock of hair off his forehead. "You're not even my type."

"You've told me this before. What exactly is your type?" he asked, his body poised, waiting.

"No three-piece suits. No Italian shoes. No gold watch." She let her fingers slide through his thick silky hair. "No fancy haircuts or blow-dryers or afternoon squash games at the club."

"Think you've got me pegged, don't you, Maggie?"

"Oh, yes," she breathed as his arms went around her once again. "You're everything I don't want in a man."

"I don't stand a chance?"

Oh, God, how wonderful his hands felt against her back, so warm, so strong. So incredibly, savagely male. "No chance at all."

"Then you wouldn't mind if I kissed you to find out what I'm losing?"

"Be my guest."

Famous last words.

He brought his face closer to hers, then closer still, until only the sweet scent of champagne and raspberries separated them. Her lips parted in anticipation. Her mouth grew lusciously moist as she waited while he took his sweet, sweet time taking what she offered.

That kiss he'd given her back on the porch of The White Elephant was a sip of sparkling wine.

But the kiss he gave her now was brandy: deep, rich, powerful. A strange and dangerous melding of the physical and the emotional that made it impossible for her to tell where the reality of the moment left off and the fantasy began.

Thank God, John Adams Tyler wasn't her type.

JOHN WAS IN TROUBLE.

Big trouble.

The hot wet feel of her mouth, the sounds she made deep in her throat, the yielding softness of her shoulders and arms—they were taking him someplace he wasn't ready to go.

Not yet.

Mindless seduction wasn't the name of this game.

He didn't want their first time to be quick or thoughtless or something to be remembered later with anything but joy.

But if he didn't pull away from Maggie within the next half second, all his good intentions would go up in flames.

He broke the kiss, and it took a full minute before he could control his respiration well enough to speak. He got to his feet and held out his hand. "Let's go."

She blinked as if awakening from a dream. "Go?"

"Leave," he said, wishing she didn't look so ripe, so accessible. "You have an early morning, remember?"

She brought his wrist closer and peered dazedly at his watch. "I still have time."

He took her hand and helped her to her feet. "You're going home, Maggie." He retrieved her shoes from under the chair. "Put these on."

She stared at him as if he spoke a foreign tongue. "You're throwing me out?"

He bent down to slip her shoes onto her narrow-boned feet and resisted the urge to run his tongue across her instep.

"I'm throwing you out."

Her lips were rosy and swollen from his kisses, her hair tumbled crazily over her shoulders and back. The top of her dress had shifted slightly off center, exposing the delicate lines of her right collarbone and the lacy strap of her bra.

All in all, he'd never seen a more beautiful, more desirable woman in his entire life.

"I don't understand."

"You will when you think about it tomorrow, Maggie." Maybe then she could explain it to him.

"I hate riddles," she said, following him back down the hallway toward the staircase. "You tell me I'm the woman you want to marry, then you throw me out of your bedroom. You *are* crazy."

He thought about the way she'd felt in his arms. "You're right," he said, taking her hand as she stumbled at the top step. "I probably am."

She came to an abrupt stop. "Will you slow down, for heaven's sake? Being thrown out is bad enough—I don't want a broken ankle in the bargain."

He looked down at her strappy high heels. The longer it took to put some distance between himself and temptation, the greater the chances he would succumb.

He swept her up into his arms and continued down the stairs.

"You've got it all wrong," she said, starting to laugh. "Rhett carried Scarlett *up* the staircase, not *down*."

"This is the eighties," he said grimly. "We make our own traditions."

She curled her left arm around his neck, and her right hand rested lightly against his chest. "My hero!" She was laughing so hard her words were difficult to understand. "Saving me from my own baser instincts. You didn't have to, you know."

He said nothing, just continued down the stairs.

"I wasn't going to ravish you, John," she said, obviously finding the situation hilarious. "You're not even my type."

He didn't believe that, not for a minute, but this wasn't the time to debate that particular issue. She'd admit the truth sooner or later.

"You can trust me, John," she continued. "Cross my heart and hope to die."

He stopped at the bottom of the last flight of stairs, leaned back against the railing and looked deep into her eyes. "You can't trust me, Maggie," he said and then proceeded to prove that statement to her with his mouth and hands.

She was quiet when he put her down, but he knew by her rapid breathing and flushed cheeks that she'd been as affected by what they'd shared as he.

"I'll walk you to your car," he said, taking her hand.

"Fine," she said, her voice unsteady. "I'd like that."

The lobby was empty except for the night clerk who sat behind the reception desk working a crossword puzzle and watching David Letterman on a portable TV propped up on a bookshelf.

John nodded at the man and marched toward the front door. Maggie seemed to not even notice the clerk's existence. She was quiet, almost contemplative, and he'd give half his fortune to know what she was thinking.

Of course, if he was lucky, he'd learn soon enough.

It was quiet outside save for the buzz of the crickets and the faint sounds of music from the nightclub on the south side of the property. The curving driveway was awash with moonlight and, for once, it seemed all the newlyweds were someplace else.

He didn't even feel ridiculous as he strode toward her car, which was parked in the visitor's lot behind the main building.

He was too much in love to feel anything but the thrill of holding her close.

They reached her car, and he lifted her on the front fender and, arms still around him, she brought her mouth toward his for another kiss.

"What was that for?" he asked, too dizzy to pay attention to the crunch of leaves behind him.

"Making sure," she whispered, kissing him again. "I had to make sure you weren't my type."

"And you're positive?"

She nodded. "Absolutely. I'm in no danger, John."

He leaned over her. "Glad to hear it," he said as her hands caressed the muscles of his shoulders. "I wouldn't want you to be in any danger."

He lowered his mouth toward hers for one last kiss before he sent her back to The White Elephant. Her breath was sweet and warm and—

Hold it!

Three motorcycles—huge mean motorcycles, not those pastel versions that were sprouting everywhere like dandelions—were angled across the outer edge of the driveway.

And leaning against those motorcycles were three misplaced Hell's Angels who looked as out of place in front of Hideaway Haven as John had felt in the Bronze Penguin.

The tallest of the three had jet-black hair slicked off his forehead in an eighties version of a D.A. A pack of cigarettes bulged from the short sleeve of his white T-shirt.

A shorter, more muscular blond man with a diamond stud in his right ear struck a match against the sole of his boot and lit a Marlboro.

The one with the blaze of unruly red hair and a leather jacket straight out of *The Wild Bunch* stepped forward.

"Get in the car," John said to Maggie.

"What?" She still had the sleepy look of a woman waiting to be kissed. "I thought—"

"Don't think," he ordered. "Just listen. Get in the car and leave." He wasn't ready for the collision of past and future. Not yet.

"John, I—"

He pulled her off the front fender, opened the car door and unceremoniously pushed her inside.

"I'll call you."

He'd have to. This wasn't exactly the way to woo your future wife.

The red-haired man stopped about ten feet away from John.

"You're a tough man to track down," he said, all menace and muscle. "We figured home turf was our best bet."

John reached inside his breast pocket for a cigarette before remembering he no longer smoked. Damn.

"I need more time." He glanced over at the other two men as they approached. "You didn't think I'd run out on you, did you?"

The other time it had been different. No one could have blamed him for running as long and far as a broken heart could carry him.

"Hey, man, we didn't know what to think. You backed out on lunch, didn't you?"

"I left you a message." He was glad he wasn't wearing his suit. The trappings of corporate success would have put him at a disadvantage with this particular group. "You're asking a lot of me. I need more time to think."

"Time's up," the red-haired man said, drawing closer. "We need your answer now."

The Russells from Ohio and the Matamores from Philadelphia stopped at the foot of the driveway on their way to the nightclub, took one look at the group assembled near John, then headed abruptly back toward their cottages, as if coming face-to-face with a crazed grizzly were preferable to a showdown with these middle-aged motorcycle jockeys.

"You're scaring the paying customers," John said, aware that Maggie was still in the car behind him.

"Can't have that," said the red-haired man. "Can't let our leader lose money, can we?"

John bristled. "You're pushin', Terry," he warned, his accent reverting back to the Brooklyn street corner where he'd learned about life. "I'll answer when I answer."

"You'll answer now," said Terry. "One way or the other, it's time you made up your mind. Are you with us or not?"

He'd avoided it for too long—he saw that now.

In the faces of the men before him, he saw his own aging in a way his mirror didn't catch. He had the time and the money for personal trainers and hand-tailored clothes and vacations to Gstaad to recharge his batteries.

Life had been damned good to him since that day he walked out on these men and, one way or the other, it was time he did something for the guys who'd been there back when they were all young and hungry and so innocent.

Maybe you couldn't go back home again, but John Adams Tyler hoped like hell you could visit.

"You in?" Terry asked, raising his fists in their old way of cementing an agreement, the way of their streets.

John matched the other man's body language as if it had been yesterday and not fifteen years ago. "If you beat me, you get me."

They circled each other warily as the other men cheered them on.

John waited until Terry threw the first punch, and that's when all hell broke loose.

## Chapter Eleven

One minute Maggie was in John's arms thinking how she'd been too hasty in declaring he wasn't her type, and the next minute she was behind the wheel of her battered Jeep Cherokee, while John faced three Hell's Angels by himself.

Her car windows were rolled up, so she couldn't hear what the red-haired man was saying to John, but she didn't need to.

Body language was enough.

The man with the red hair raised his fists.

Tyler's fists clenched in response.

They circled each other. Then before she could scream out a warning, the redhead in the leather jacket broke rank and headed straight for Tyler.

One of the things Maggie had learned during her years with PAX was to recognize trouble when she saw it.

Fortunately for John, she'd also learned how to deal with it. Judo, karate and plain down-and-dirty street fighting had all been part of her training.

Who would have thought she'd save his life twice in two days?

She kicked off her heels and leaped out of the car. The blacktop stung her bare feet as she ran full speed toward the brawling men.

She was at the man's throat in a flash, eight years of forgotten martial arts training resurfacing in the blink of an eye.

John's attacker let out a howl and hit the ground, butt first. Maggie dug her knee into his chest.

"Check for weapons," she snapped to John as she glared at the other Hell's Angels. The blond man took a step toward her. "One more move, and your pal is history."

What in hell was the matter with Tyler? He stood there, mouth open, gaping at her like some sort of village idiot.

"Check for weapons," she ordered as she began to frisk the man on the ground, "then call the cops."

"The cops!" The man on the ground yelped as she dug her knee in even deeper. "What the hell's going on?"

"Woman's crazy." The man with the blond hair backed away, palms up in surrender. "Won't catch me near her."

"Call her off, Tyler," said the hood with the cigarette bulge in his T-shirt. "She's ruinin' all our fun."

Maggie looked up at John who still hadn't moved an inch. "You know these punks?"

He shook his head. "Never saw them before in my life."

Was that the reflection of the gas lamps lining the drive, or a definite twinkle in his golden eyes?

"Out with it, Tyler," she said. "This isn't funny."

"Yeah," said the guy on the ground. "This ain't one damned bit funny."

"From where I stand, it is."

"Well, I ain't standin', Tyler, and I sure as hell ain't laughin'."

Maggie loosened her hold on the man's throat, and her fingers started to itch for John's. "In case you haven't noticed, Tyler, I'm not laughing, either."

"Let him up, Maggie," he said with an easy grin. "I know him."

There was no easy way to do it. Maggie's knee dug into the poor man's chest one last time as she stood up— without Tyler's help, she couldn't help but notice.

"You owe me an explanation," she hissed in Tyler's direction as she turned to storm back toward her car. "I'm humiliated."

She heard him say something to the three men. She heard their laughter, low and slightly nervous, then the sound of Tyler himself coming after her.

"Who *are* those people?" she asked when he caught up with her. "They look like hoods."

"I have to tell them that," he said. "They'll like it."

"You still haven't answered me." She pulled her car keys out of her bag.

"We grew up together."

She arched a brow. "And they say hello by starting a fight?"

"It's an old ritual." He narrowed his eyes, "Where are you from?"

"Effingham, Illinois."

He laughed. "You'd never understand."

"Try me," she said. "I'm a lot smarter than you think."

He tugged at the neck of his sweater as if it were his red silk tie. "We used to sing together."

"Sing?" Her earlier suspicions about him were beginning to seem more absurd by the minute.

"One of those street-corner groups that were popular in the sixties."

She searched her memory for a name. "Like Dion and the Belmonts?"

"Younger," he said dryly. "And more successful."

She started to ask if they'd ever made a record when he smoothly moved in front of her, blocking the door of her car.

"You realize what you just did, don't you?" he asked.

He would zero back in on that. "Sure I do. I've made a total fool of myself in front of three strangers." She tried to push him out of the way, but he wouldn't budge. This didn't seem the time to whip out any more of her martial arts training.

"You saved my life again, Maggie. I don't know where the hell you got those moves, but you were pretty damned impressive."

"Big deal," she said. "So I took a few karate lessons."

"It *is* a big deal. You used it to save my life again."

"No, I didn't," she protested weakly. "You know those guys. You weren't in any danger—you said so yourself."

"But *you* didn't know that."

No man should look that good by moonlight.

She gathered her composure. "I fail to see what difference that makes."

"You thought I was in trouble, and you came to my rescue." His breath brushed her cheek, wonderfully warm despite the cool night. "I see a definite pattern emerging."

"So do I," she said. "I'm a jerk."

"Admit it, Maggie Douglass. You're having second thoughts about me."

"I'm having second thoughts about my sanity." The truth was, she found herself wishing she was back upstairs in that crazy room with his mouth against hers. "I should have left you there on the floor of the Bronze Penguin and been done with it."

"Look me in the eye and say that."

She hesitated and glanced over at the three men standing near the motorcycles.

"Last chance, Maggie. If you can look me in the eye and say that, I won't bother you again."

What was the use? She closed her eyes and rested her forehead against his shoulder. "Damn you, Tyler," she whispered. "You know I can't."

"That's what I was hoping."

He put his hands on her shoulders and pushed her away until their eyes met.

"Why fight it, Maggie? It's in the stars."

"You're crazy, Tyler." Funny and gorgeous, but totally, unmistakably mad. "You don't know anything about me."

"I'll learn," he said, his fingers tangling once again in her hair. "I can't think of a better way to spend the rest of my life."

A flip remark, sophisticated and witty, died on her lips as it finally hit her. "You mean this, don't you?"

"You finally realized it?"

"I think so."

"And?"

He was gently massaging her scalp, and she found it increasingly difficult to think.

"And I think I'd better go home." Before she found herself on a plane bound for Las Vegas and one of those wedding chapels on the Strip.

"Breakfast tomorrow?"

"Can't. I work for a living, remember?"

"Lunch."

"John, the staff. I—"

He pressed his index finger against her lips. "Dinner. After the rush is over. No excuses."

"Dinner," she answered. She couldn't come up with one good excuse to keep herself away from him.

He opened the car door, and as Maggie climbed inside she realized that tonight, somewhere between the champagne and the water bed, John Adams Tyler had become exactly her type of man.

Which was wonderful except for the fact that last night she'd promised her uncle three things: no publicity, no strangers bearing gifts and no romantic entanglements.

In just twenty-four hours she'd found herself on the front page of the *Pocono Bugle*, the recipient of a million dollars in funny money, and now it looked as if she were headed for the most romantic entanglement of her entire life.

Another woman would call Alistair up and say, "Sorry, Uncle. Maybe another time."

Unfortunately, that wasn't Maggie's speed.

Her loyalty to her uncle ran deep, and the thought of what the Summit could mean to The White Elephant, deeper still.

She'd spent the better part of her life doing what was right, doing what she promised, doing what she was told. Responsibility had always been her strong suit and, damn it, no matter how much she wished it could be otherwise, this time was no exception.

She sighed and started the engine.

She hoped Tyler was a patient man because starting tomorrow, she would have to put him on hold.

JOHN WAITED until Maggie disappeared around the curving driveway before he faced his old friends.

They were grinning and nudging each other just the way they used to back in high school, and John felt the same goofy kind of embarrassment he'd felt at seventeen.

"Say one word, and you're dead men," he said as he crossed the blacktop to where they stood.

"He talks tough," said Terry, his red hair bristling. "Think he means it?"

Frankie and Joe gave him the once-over.

"Nah," said Frankie, still the street punk with the angel face. "We're his buddies."

"Yeah," said Joe, whose blond hair was liberally laced with gray. "And buddies get to know everything, right?"

"Wrong," said John. "I'll talk about the old days with you. I'll talk about business. But don't ask me anything about Maggie. She's off-limits."

A lot of years had gone by since they were the four musketeers, and John wasn't up to pretending things hadn't changed.

He owed them something, sure, but he didn't owe them this.

Maggie, and how she made him feel, was too important to trivialize.

The three men fell silent, and the silence stretched until John became acutely aware of the sound of his own breathing. It was an old street game, the same game played in corporate boardrooms across the nation each and every day.

A game of emotional chicken where the first one who broke the silence gave himself away.

He had won so often in the boardroom that he could afford to lose this one time.

"Okay," he said, breaking the silence and giving them control, "where were we?"

Their relief was almost palpable.

"The concert's set for two weeks from tomorrow." Terry adjusted the collar of his jacket.

"The deal's already made?"

"Signed, sealed and almost delivered."

Frankie's cigarette glowed red in the darkness. "That's where you come in, Johnny."

Terry shot Frankie a look, and the dark-haired man took another drag on his cigarette and fell silent.

"I'll give it to you straight," said Terry, hands in the pockets of his leather jacket. "Without you, we don't have a deal."

"Come on," John said, suddenly uncomfortable. "You guys went on for years without me and did great." He remembered two gold records that he wished had been his. "Why the sudden interest in me?"

"Seems to me a smart guy like you could figure that out," said Joe. He didn't say much as a rule, but when he did it was worth listening. "Times change. The sixties took its toll. Most of the groups weren't as lucky as we were."

The list Joe recited was long and heartbreaking: the Beatles without John Lennon; The Mamas and the Papas without the ebullient Cass; the Doors without Jim Morrison. Rolling Stones. Supremes. Temptations. All had lost an original member.

Even the Beach Boys, those eternally golden teenagers, had lost one of their own to the California surf that made them famous long ago.

"They want all of us, Johnny, or the deal's off." Terry looked him straight in the eye. "You owe us a farewell performance."

A farewell performance. The performance he'd denied them when he'd tossed it all aside that August night.

The one time in his life when John had taken the easy way out and now, fifteen years later, it was coming back to haunt him.

"The whole group will perform?" he asked, knowing the answer as well as he knew the sound of his own voice.

"The whole group," said Terry, not backing down. "Just the way it was."

But of course that was a lie. Nothing was just the way it was.

For years John had believed it all behind him, part of another life he barely remembered.

Now that he was on the verge of something wonderful with Maggie, it was time to prove it to himself, once and for all.

"It's going to mean a lot of rehearsing, won't it?"

Terry nodded.

"Madison Square Garden?"

Terry nodded again. "Sellout crowd."

"Top billing?"

Terry's manic Irish grin spread across his face. "Is there any other way to fly?"

"What the hell," John said finally. "I probably still have my bell-bottoms in the attic."

"We can count on you?" The look of naked hope in Terry's eyes made John realize just how far and long he'd traveled from the man he used to be.

"You can count on me." He wondered how Maggie would feel about being a groupie.

Get out the love beads and light the incense: The Domino Theory was back in business.

"I'M ASHAMED OF YOU, Alistair." Holland's voice seemed loud in the silent Rolls. "Spying on your own niece."

"Spying is an ugly word," he said as they watched Maggie's car turn into the driveway of The White Elephant. "I wanted to make certain she got back safely."

"Got back safely?" What on earth was the matter with the man? "She went down the road for dinner, not to Afghanistan."

"She didn't seem herself this afternoon, and I was concerned."

"If you're so concerned, why don't you speak with her? It makes more sense than hiding here in the dark waiting for her to come home."

Holland tried to resist the urge to light another cigarette. She was doing her best to live without decadent treats like Gauloises, but it was proving more difficult than she would have imagined.

Living without Alistair didn't bear thinking about.

"You almost had me fooled," she continued. "I actually believed you wanted one more moonlight tryst before we went back to the big, bad city."

"If memory serves, a good time was had by all."

The darkness hid her eyes from his, and for that she was eternally grateful. Vulnerability wasn't something she was proud of. "If memory serves, I was the one who was had."

She heard his slow intake of breath, and she knew she'd hit upon the truth.

"I know this must seem ridiculous to you, Holland—"

"Damn straight," she muttered under her breath.

"—but family dynamics are difficult to explain to an outsider."

*As usual, my darling, your aim is superb.*

"Oh, yes," she said, her voice sharp as his profile, "I doubt if I could fathom the complexities of the Chambers family dynamics. I am, after all, just a simple country maiden."

"You do yourself an injustice, Holland."

"No, my darling, you do me the injustice." She was tired of the secrets. Tired of the double-talk. Tired of the strange happenings accompanied by even stranger explanations.

Hell, she was tired of coming in second and not knowing who, or what, was coming in first.

She'd learned a lot about herself this weekend.

She'd learned it was time to think about herself.

She glanced at Alistair and tried to ignore the way her heart ached.

"It's a long drive," she said, leaning her head back against the seat rest and closing her eyes, "and I have an early-morning call."

Alistair said nothing. He simply started up the Rolls and headed back to Manhattan.

And that, to Holland, said it all.

# Chapter Twelve

The only light in the room was the phosphorescent glow from the computer screen.

*Enter data.*

*Enter data.*

Alistair had been staring at that screen for an endless time, alternating between drags on his cigarette and deep gulps of black coffee sent in from the all-night delicatessen on the next block.

Three hours ago he'd dropped Holland off at her apartment on the West Side. They'd barely spoken on the drive back from the Poconos. He knew she had her questions, a thousand of them, but he also knew that answers were something he couldn't give.

He thought he'd find escape in work, but so far he had accomplished nothing.

The details surrounding the Summit were endless, and his time was growing short.

He had to but press a few of the keys before him and the amazing machinery of PAX would spring to life, ready to transform Maggie's White Elephant into a place worthy of its spot in history.

Why, then, was he staring out at the street lamps on Fifth Avenue and working his way through his second packet of cigarettes?

He ground one out in the marble ashtray on the window ledge, typed in the words *Honeymoon Hotel*, then sat back and waited while the computer accessed PAX's master file.

"...I was the one who was had."

Holland's words beat against his heart like a sledge.

*Truth hurts, doesn't it, old man?*

PAX.

The mistress that kept him from drawing Holland closer and letting what existed between them flower and grow.

Sarah had understood, but then his Sarah had danced to the same tune, heard the same seductive music that had lured sailors better than he onto the rocks.

Holland was a woman with needs of her own. Ambitions that were finally being realized.

He couldn't ask her to fling everything aside and join him in this rootless, dangerous existence predicated on half truths.

Tonight he'd made a grievous error: he'd let his personal life cloud his professional judgment. He'd blurred the lines that had once been sharply etched, and Holland had been badly hurt in the process.

The computer screen blazed to life.

*Choice.*

It always came down to choice.

He and Sarah had faced them.

As had Maggie, in her way.

Ryder and Joanna.

A thousand others whose names he didn't know, but whose stories were all too familiar.

Nothing would change the reality of his situation.

As long as he remained within the organization, nothing *could* change it.

But that was neither here nor there.

The Summit Meeting was but a few weeks away, and for now he knew where his loyalties must rest.

But after the Summit was over—

Well, if the Fates and Holland Masters were both on his side, PAX would be in for a surprise.

MAGGIE DIDN'T SLEEP that night. Every time she closed her eyes a vision of mirrored ceilings danced through her champagne-saturated brain.

Funny thing—John was reflected in every one of them.

If he was a spy, he was a pretty bad one, because last night he could have had every last PAX secret she knew just for the asking.

Maybe it was this whole bizarre thing with Alistair and The White Elephant and that incredible Summit Meeting that had her seeing trouble around every corner. She didn't want to think that John was anything more than what he seemed to be: an extraordinarily successful businessman who made her heart beat faster and kept her up all night thinking crazy thoughts.

About six she gave up the ghost. She took a shower in an attempt to look alive, made some coffee and did her best to ignore Groucho's screeching from his cage in her office.

She was nursing her third cup at the kitchen table when Rachel found her.

"Good grief, honey! You look terrible." Rachel was never one to mince words. "I hope that's a good sign."

"You have a voice that could cut through lead," Maggie said, rubbing her throbbing temples. "Why didn't I ever notice that before?"

Rachel sat down at the table and poured herself a cup of coffee. "A hangover? I don't believe it."

"It's not a hangover," Maggie protested grimly. "I didn't sleep."

"I think it's a hangover."

"I only had three glasses of champagne, Rachel. That's hardly the lost weekend."

"So he serves champagne, does he?" Rachel leaned back in her chair, looking extremely smug. "Mr. Tyler lives up to expectations."

"What does that mean?"

"Oh, come on, honey. I'm not blind."

Maggie took a long gulp of coffee. "You've been watching too many soaps, Rae." Rachel believed in fairy tales and fantasies and undying love.

"Don't change the subject."

Maggie sighed. "You hopeless romantics are too damned single-minded." John Adams Tyler was living proof of that.

"This is even better than I hoped. Tyler is a hopeless romantic, too?"

"I must be crazy," Maggie muttered. "You're the last person on earth I should be talking to about this. You're my mother-in-law."

Rachel patted her hand. "I'm your friend. I want to see you happy."

"I am happy."

"Not happy enough to suit me."

Maggie tossed a packet of Equal at her. "You've been happily married for almost forty years. If you knew what it was like out there, you wouldn't set me up on so many blind dates."

"It's no different than it ever was, honey. Human nature doesn't change."

"That's where you're wrong, Rae. Things move a lot faster these days."

"Blame your age, Maggie, not society."

"My age? What does age have to do with anything?"

Rachel ignored Maggie's scowl and lit a cigarette. "It's the law of diminishing returns."

"Great," said Maggie, fanning the smoke back at Rachel with her napkin. "It's eight in the morning. I'm lucky if I got forty-five minutes sleep last night, and I have a headache that's playing the 'Anvil Chorus' inside my brain. I don't need riddles."

"No riddles," said Rachel, blithely puffing away. "The older you get, the less time you have left. You tend to make quicker judgments."

Maggie shivered. "How depressing. You've given love at first sight a whole new meaning."

"Not really. All I'm saying is, why waste time when you already know what you want?"

"That's assuming you know what you want. Life isn't always that simple."

"Love is."

"Another quote from the gospel according to hopeless romantics?"

"Another quote from a woman who loves you like a daughter."

Tears, sudden and hot, welled up in Maggie's eyes, and she blinked rapidly. "Unfair, Rachel. Pulling rank is beneath you."

"I've known you a long time, honey. You're like one of my own." She stroked Maggie's hair, then patted her gently on the shoulder. "And I know more about you than you think."

Maggie stiffened. "Such as?"

Rachel stubbed out her cigarette and looked Maggie straight in the eye. "You think I don't know the truth about you and my son?"

Maggie snapped her fingers, praying she looked nonchalant. "Darn! You found out about the UFO in the backyard."

Rachel didn't crack a smile. "I know how it was between the two of you."

"Look, Rachel, I don't know what you're driving at, but it's time for me to start breakfast for the masses." She went to stand up, but Rachel's hand on her forearm stopped her.

"Before Rick died he told me."

Maggie waited, her heart thudding painfully. "Told you what?"

Rachel's eyes were filled with compassion. "That you two had filed for divorce."

Maggie dismissed it with a wave of her hand. "Old news, Rae. Why, we—"

"He also told me you withdrew the papers when you found out he had cancer."

Rachel had her dead to rights.

"He needed a good friend," Maggie said quietly. "He would have done as much for me."

"Not many women would have done what you did, Maggie."

Maggie mumbled something about being loyal as a sheepdog, but Rachel stopped her again midsentence.

"Loyalty's a rare commodity these days, honey. I just hope you don't have loyalty to Rick all tied up with this damned inn and—"

Maggie cracked six eggs into a huge copper bowl and reached for the tin of cinnamon. "Believe it or not, I love this damned inn, Rae. I want it to be a success." Three or four years ago her motives had indeed been all tied up with Rick and her sorrow and guilt, but not any longer.

She'd grown deeply attached to the rambling main house and the sprawling grounds, and the challenge of turning it into something special appealed to her sense of the absurd.

"I know you, honey," Rachel said. "You've always had a soft spot for the underdog."

Maggie named the last two blind dates Rachel and George had sent her out on. "Tell me about it!"

"I'm talking about The White Elephant."

"I'll admit we have an image problem."

Rachel's look was sly. "Nothing a few mirrored ceilings couldn't cure."

Maggie winced at the memory of how she'd looked as she struggled to escape the clutches of John's huge water bed last night. "Mirrored ceilings aren't all that great."

Rachel's eyes twinkled merrily. "Do tell! Maybe I can leave for vacation with a happy heart after all."

"Just don't go mailing me any Vikings, Rae."

Her mother-in-law's laugh had Maggie clutching her temples. "If you promise me you won't elope before I get back."

Maggie crossed her heart with a wire whisk. "You have my word. Now get to work!"


IT WAS HOLLAND'S first morning back in Manhattan, and she was spending it at the O'Neals' apartment at the Carillon, the place where she'd first met Alistair Chambers.

All night long she'd tossed and turned, trying vainly to make sense out of Alistair's bizarre behavior.

There was only one person on earth who would understand her confusion. Joanna Stratton O'Neal, who'd shared the puzzle with Holland since the very beginning, might have the answer she was looking for.

"He did *what*?" Joanna's turquoise eyes were wide as she stared across the table at Holland.

Holland looked up from her croissant. "You heard me. He spied on his own niece."

"Maggie?"

"He has another one?"

Joanna put her cup down and shook her head. "Why would he hide in the bushes and spy on Maggie?"

Holland polished off her croissant and reached for another. "I was hoping you could tell me."

"Me? I barely know the woman. I have no idea what she could be up to."

"It's not what she's up to that worries me, Jo." She split the croissant and piled it shamelessly high with butter and raspberry jam. "Unless I miss my guess, it has something to do with Alistair and Ryder and whatever it is the two of them do."

Joanna's expression grew guarded, the way it always did when Holland raised that particular subject. "I think you're letting your imagination run away with you, Holland. You know they're in finance."

Holland bit back a curse. "I was in the car with him, Joanna. I saw him do it."

"Maybe Alistair is worried about her," Joanna suggested. "Maybe he doesn't like the man she's seeing, and he wanted to make certain she got home safely."

"That's exactly what Alistair said."

Joanna brightened. "See? I knew there must be a simple explanation. Why do you always look for things that aren't there?"

Holland glared at her friend. "I liked you better when you were dressed like an old lady and trying to figure Ryder and Alistair out. You're too well trained for my taste now."

Joanna pushed her chair back and got to her feet. "Now what the hell does that mean?"

"It means you've changed, Jo. From the day you and Ryder came back from that mysterious trip with Alistair—after keeping me waiting for two days, I might add—you've been different."

"Marriage does that." Joanna's voice was low, controlled. "I have new responsibilities."

"It's more than that." Holland would never forget that long, aching weekend when it had seemed Maggie, Joanna and Ryder had all vanished from the face of the earth. Two years later Holland was still waiting for an explanation she could believe. "You're in with them, aren't you?"

"I don't know what you're talking about."

Holland finished her second croissant, and only the thought of her wardrobe mistress's wrath kept her from demolishing a third. "I think you do."

"You think wrong, Holland. I'm a makeup artist, same as I ever was."

"Then why aren't you working?"

Joanna sat back down. "I am working."

"Afraid not, darling. Benny Ryan says he hasn't seen you in months."

"I work for a lot of people besides Benny Ryan, Holland. Perhaps he's feeling slighted."

Holland ticked off all the other people her best friend had once worked with. "They're all feeling slighted, Jo. What gives?"

"Don't ask questions I can't answer."

"Don't patronize me," Holland retorted.

"Speak to Alistair." Joanna pushed her shiny black hair off her face and met Holland's eyes. "Tell him how you feel."

Exasperated, Holland grabbed for the third croissant, wardrobe mistress be damned.

"I'm going to find out what's going on, Jo," she warned as she picked up the knife. "Sooner or later, I'm going to find out everything."

RACHEL STAYED ON through the breakfast rush, even though she and George were leaving that night for their Scandinavian vacation. Strange, but if John hadn't come into her life, Maggie might have taken them up on their invitation while The White Elephant was making history.

Alistair called twice while they were frying the French toast, and Maggie had somehow managed to deflect Rachel's curiosity by keeping her end of the conversation as bland and boring as possible.

"Your uncle is a fascinating man, but a real mystery," Rachel said after Maggie hung up for the second time. "First we don't see him around here for ages, and now he and Holland are permanent fixtures."

"Well, they're not permanent fixtures around here," Maggie said, trying to reroute Rachel's curiosity. "They seem to like the decor at Hideaway Haven better."

"Progress," said Rachel, piling French toast up on a plate. "You're not calling it the pleasure palace anymore."

"Don't go reading anything into that now, Rae," she warned. "Maybe I'm searching for a new nickname."

Rachel, of course, remained unconvinced and continued to extol the virtues of Mr. Tyler whom she had never met, until Maggie regretted ever changing the topic from her uncle Alistair.

Finally when breakfast was over, Maggie shooed Rachel off with a hug and a promise to drop by later and see them off just as Alistair called for the third time.

"When do the last of your guests check out?"

"They'll be gone by noon."

She heard the sound of keystrokes in the background.

"Our people will be there by two o'clock, Maggie." He quoted some figures. "Are those the dimensions of your property?"

"I think so. If you like, I can run into my office and hunt up the paperwork—that is, if it isn't in the bottom of Groucho's cage."

"What a marvelous businesswoman." His tone was unusually acerbic even for the wry Alistair. "I hesitate to ask where you keep your bankbooks."

"That's one of the benefits of being flat broke, Ally. I don't have to worry about things like that."

"We'll access county records for your property lines," he said briskly. "I would hate for you to disturb that winged creature of yours."

Maggie knew there was no love lost between her uncle and her parrot, but usually Alistair made a joke of their terrible relationship.

"Are you okay, Alistair?"

He missed a beat. "Of course, Magdalena."

*Too late, Uncle. You gave yourself away.*

"Is Holland back at work?"

"I assume so."

Maggie sank into a kitchen chair. So much for the course of true love.

Alistair moved smoothly to talk of business. He had arranged for an extra four weeks' paid vacation for her staff. The phone calls had been made from PAX's New York City office earlier that morning.

The first of the work crews would be there this afternoon.

All she had to do was sit back, put her feet up and relax until the Summit was over.

In fact, most of her relaxing would be done on the deck of Alistair's yacht, *La Jolie*, which she would be meeting in Bermuda the day before the Summit began.

No worries.

No cares.

No more sloppy joes to make.

And, if she was true to the letter of the agreement, no more John Adams Tyler until the Summit was over.

It was a small price to pay for all the wonders promised her.

Wasn't it?

Suddenly Maggie wasn't so sure. Rachel was a shrewd woman, and she had zeroed in on Maggie's heart with the same precision as one of PAX's laser beam weapons.

What John made her feel was something brand-new. Something she'd never known in the arms of her husband.

*Face facts, Douglass. Everyone knew it before you did.*

Even Sarah.

SARAH CHAMBERS wasn't well.

Maggie Stewart had been denying it for a long time, but she could deny it no longer. Her aunt's usual brisk stride had slowed to a cautious walk that was painful to watch. Hair that had once been glossy and black as ebony was now flat and laced with streaks of gray darker than a stormy sky. Her high, elegant cheekbones were angry slashes in a face growing thinner every day.

Maggie rose from her easy chair and enfolded her aunt's spare frame in an embrace. "You didn't have to come downstairs, Sarah," she said, taking Sarah's arm and helping her to the chair by the window. "We could have chatted up in your bedroom."

"You young people," Sarah said fondly as she settled herself in her chair. "No respect for the proprieties. How can I serve you tea in my bedroom?"

"Uh-oh." Maggie sat down opposite her aunt. "That means I'm in for a serious conversation, doesn't it?"

Sarah poured for each of them. "Yes it does, Maggie. Marriage is a serious topic." Her eyes, green as the Irish countryside beyond the window, were filled with love and concern.

When Maggie had announced she would be leaving PAX, there had been the expected uproar from Alistair. "Do you understand what you're leaving, Magdalena?" he had demanded. "In your lifetime, you'll never have an opportunity such as PAX again."

She had just laughed and kissed his cheek. While the work was fun, it wasn't her life. She wanted to go to sleep in the same place night after night. She wanted a home and a husband and a family and everything that went with it.

And more than anything, she had wanted her aunt and uncle to share her happiness.

Until this moment, she thought they did.

"I don't understand, Sarah. I thought you liked Rick and his family."

Just two months before, Alistair and Sarah had flown to Pennsylvania to meet Rick's family, and the occasion had been everything Maggie could have hoped for. Even though the Douglass family owned three hotels in elite Bucks County and Rick owned a country inn deep in the Poconos, they had opened their home to Alistair and Sarah and welcomed them as their own, the same way they had welcomed Maggie into the fold.

"We do like them indeed. The Douglasses are wonderful people. We couldn't have asked for a better family to join with ours."

"Then what's the problem?" Maggie, at twenty-three, was not known for patience or subtlety. "The wedding is next month. This is a heck of a time to tell me you—"

Sarah's laugh was sweet and clear. "How impatient you are, my girl. How very like your mother."

Maggie smiled despite herself. "You have me on pins and needles, Sarah." Suddenly her smile froze. "Don't tell me you won't be able to make it to Pennsylvania for the wedding!" She'd have to be blind to not see that Sarah's illness was rapidly progressing.

Sarah reached for her hand and squeezed. "I'll be there if I have to charter my own plane to get me there."

"You and Alistair are like parents to me. I couldn't imagine getting married without you two there with me."

Sarah passed a hand over her eyes. "I don't know how to begin this, Maggie."

"Is something wrong? Are you...?" Her words drifted away. The thought of Sarah leaving her one day was more than Maggie could handle.

"Don't worry, darling. I'll be around a long time yet."

"Then what is it? Why do you look so serious? Weddings are wonderful! You should be happy for me."

Sarah's green eyes never left Maggie's. "Are *you*?"

"Am I what?" She tugged at her plaid skirt and tried to settle back in the chair.

"Are you happy?"

Maggie waved her left hand, the one with the beautiful engagement ring sparkling on it. "Of course, I'm happy. I'm engaged to be married to a wonderful man."

"Rick *is* a wonderful man," Sarah said, "but I'm concerned."

Maggie threw her head back and laughed. "Oh, don't worry about The White Elephant, Sarah. I know it looks a disaster now, but you should see the plans Rick has for it. In a few years we'll be the biggest and best hotel in the Poconos. Rick says we'll give Cove Haven a run for its money." And until then he had an independent income that, while not huge, was substantial enough to keep them this side of the poverty line.

"I'm sure you have some marvelous plans, darling, but that's not what concerns me." Sarah leaned forward, her eyes still focused intently upon her niece. "Do you love him?"

Blood rushed to Maggie's cheeks, and she could feel the heat as her face flushed bright red. "What kind of question is that?"

"Just answer me. Do you love him, Maggie?"

"Why else would I be marrying him?"

"There are many reasons for marriage besides love. I'd like to hear yours."

"Why did you marry Uncle Alistair?" Maggie countered indignantly.

"Because I couldn't imagine living my life without him," Sarah said, not missing a beat. "Because he was the kindest, most fascinatingly brilliant man I'd ever met." She paused and skewered Maggie with a look. "Because he made my blood run hot."

Maggie giggled nervously. "I don't know what to say," she murmured.

"And that is what I feared most." Sarah sat back in her chair. The sun streaming through the leaded panes highlighted the shadows beneath her eyes, the fragile contour of her shoulders. "Do you love him, Maggie?" she repeated quietly. "Truly love him?"

"Yes," said Maggie, looking away for a moment. "I love him very much." He was a good and true friend to her, and she found it easy to imagine them thirty years down the road, still together, still working on his plans for The White Elephant. "He needs me, Sarah. That's no small thing."

Even at twenty-three, Maggie had a history of going where she was needed.

Her first job as a teenager had been baby-sitting for a young widow with two baby girls.

Her second had been with a cousin who owned a record store and couldn't afford to pay for non-family help.

And, of course, there was PAX. She had the McBride gift. They needed it. Add a pinch of family loyalty and a lot of gratitude and voilà! Maggie became a spy.

"There's more to marriage than that, Maggie. There's passion to be considered."

"Sarah, really, I don't think we should be talking about this."

Sarah, however, was not to be deterred. "Work isn't what kept Alistair and I together all these years."

"Sarah, please! I wish you wouldn't—"

"Passion, Maggie. When the sun goes down, it's passion that keeps a man and a woman together. Don't ever let anyone tell you different."

"That's absurd," said Maggie. Sex was only part of a relationship. Everyone knew that. "Rick and I are a team, a unit. We think alike; we want the same things."

"And how does he make you feel, Maggie love, when he holds you, when he kisses you?" Sarah's eyes glittered with an intensity that made Maggie swallow hard. "You're so young, darling, way too young to compromise on something as important as your life."

"He makes me feel needed," Maggie said softly. "That's enough."

BUT, OF COURSE, it wasn't.

Sarah had known that even then.

For Maggie and Rick the realization came later on.

When they'd filed for divorce, it was more an act of friendship than anger.

Her marriage had been companionable, but that deeper commitment, that passion she'd seen at work in the best of marriages, just wasn't there.

Rachel knew that, just as Maggie and Rick had known it before his cancer was diagnosed.

Rachel, of course, was one of the lucky ones. You had only to look at Rachel and George, see the fire in their eyes, to know that sometimes you really could have it all.

She thought of how she'd felt in John's arms.

Maybe it was the real thing.

Maybe it wasn't.

But one thing was certain: she'd never know without a fight.

Maggie marched into her office. Groucho was shrieking on his perch. She climbed over the boxes of cocktail napkins and funny money, tossed the bird a peanut and reached for the telephone.

"Seven-fifty-four. Chambers."

"I want to see John Tyler, Ally."

Her uncle's sigh was loud and theatrical. "Identify yourself, please, caller."

She rummaged for the index card with her number scribbled on it. "Eight—no, make that a six. Six-seven-nine."

"Go ahead."

"Oh, come on, Ally. Don't make me repeat myself. You heard every word I said the first time."

"I rest easier each night knowing you are safely back in civilian life, my girl. Your respect for protocol leaves much to be desired."

"Protocol's a pain in the—"

"Control your temper. Our words have a habit of traveling farther afield than we might think. What is it you want?"

She took a deep breath. "I want to know if John Tyler is a spy."

"And may I ask why you want to know?"

"I know what you said about security and secrecy and everything else, Alistair, but I want to see him." *Think of something, you fool! Think of a good reason.* "I understand how important the Summit—"

"Magdalena!"

She flinched at the tone of his voice. "Sorry. I understand how important your plans are, but it seems to me, Tyler will get very suspicious if I just drop out of sight." She switched the phone to her other ear. "I mean, he might even decide to come by and . . ." Her voice trailed off ominously. "Who knows what he might see if he did."

"A valid point, Maggie."

A valid point! She stared at the phone in shock. That was Alistair's equivalent of the Pulitzer prize.

"Yes," she said coolly, "I thought so, too." She swallowed hard. "Has he been checked out yet, Alistair?" *He couldn't be a spy. The Fates wouldn't be that cruel.*

"He checked out fine, Magdalena."

Her relief was so intense that she sank down into her chair. "You're sure about that?"

"We have a dossier on Tyler, and he's on the up-and-up."

"You have a dossier on him?"

"Naturally, my girl. We have dossiers on all of your peers in the files I left behind with you."

She glanced down at the black leather pouch next to her calculator. "Full dossiers?"

"Naturally. You, of all people, should know we never employ halfway measures." He chuckled, sounding more like the Alistair she knew and loved. "Why didn't you tell me?"

"Tell you what?"

"Your Mr. Tyler is descended from American royalty."

"I don't know how to break it to you, Ally, but we have no royalty. That's why we fought that war in the first place. Taxation without representation. Fat George and his princes. Sound familiar?"

"Vaguely. Be that as it may, John and Abigail are the closest you've come to it."

"Will I be breaking the contract if I continue to see John?"

"That's a gray area, my girl."

"You've already said he's the corporate equivalent to a Boy Scout."

"I don't recall those exact words."

"He isn't a communist spy, is he?"

"No, Maggie, that he is not."

"Then if I keep him away from The White Elephant, is there a problem?"

"Technically, no."

She held back a whoop of triumph. "I have your blessing?"

"You have my permission. We'll leave blessings for those more qualified."

With those cryptic words he hung up, leaving Maggie alone with temptation.

The briefcase filled with dossiers beckoned to her.

She reached for it, then hesitated.

It seemed a gross invasion of his privacy.

*It's PAX property,* an inner voice whispered. *And you're back on the PAX payroll.*

Temptation won.

She tossed aside the files on Margo and Ernie and her other competitors even though she would have given her eyeteeth to know their fiscal forecasts.

There was only one file she wanted to see.


NAME:  John Adams Tyler   B:  3-1-53

PLACE OF BIRTH:   Brooklyn, New York
                  Flatbush section


SOPHISTICATED, ELEGANT John Adams Tyler was from Flatbush?

Incredible.

She would have guessed Park Avenue or Palm Beach.

But Brooklyn?

At least that explained those three Hell's Angels and how they figured in John's life.

She'd spent much of last night trying to figure out the connection, and the explanations she'd come up with were inventive, but inaccurate.

The real truth was even better.

Hidden beneath that perfect three-piece suit of John's was a leather jacket.

Hidden behind that corporate smile was a motorcycle maniac.

Who would have guessed he was just her type?

MARITAL STATUS: __ Married    __ Divorced

<u>X</u> Single    __ Widowed

Subject had one serious relationship between 1970 and 1973 with Laura Willis then abruptly severed the connection. Willis subsequently married and had four children.

Subject continued to—

MAGGIE TOSSED THE PAPERS facedown on her desk.

"Some spy I am," she said to Groucho who was watching her intently.

Here she had all Tyler's deep dark secrets right there at her fingertips, and she was giving up before she even made it to the juicy part.

Oh, she'd watched Oprah and Phil often enough to know that there were women who snooped through address books and men who peeked in diaries, and that the best-kept secret of the eighties was that there *were* no secrets anymore.

Government was expected to operate in the glare of the media spotlight.

Celebrities had reporters waiting at the front door of the Betty Ford Clinic for the story behind the story.

Housewives and salesmen, ex-cops and mothers of three, all vied for spots on *Good Morning America* and *Today* for the chance to tell Joan and Jane the intimate details of marriages and mastectomies, plastic surgery and plastic credit.

It was the age of information, and she had more information in front of her right at that moment than Ollie North had at the height of his intrigues.

And all of that information was about John.

Two weeks ago she would have gleefully read each and every line, praying the secrets to his success were hidden somewhere between *Height*, *Weight*, and *Religious Preference*.

She still wanted to know the secrets of his success.

That hadn't changed one bit.

What had changed was the fact that John was more to her now than the owner of half the Poconos.

He was the man she was falling in love with.

## Chapter Thirteen

PAX swooped down on The White Elephant the next morning like an avenging angel, creating order where none had ever been before.

Carpets were pulled up and whisked away to the big factory outlet in the sky. Faded wallpaper was stripped, and elegant silk patterns waited to take its place. The cottages were all treated to brand-new mattresses and bed linens of two-hundred-count percale. Windows sparkled and moldings gleamed.

And Maggie relaxed.

Well, at least she was trying to relax, but it was difficult to do much of anything with scores of workmen swarming everywhere.

She'd never seen so many drop cloths and buckets and trowels and brushes in her entire life. The inn reeked of paint and turpentine and hard work, and finally around lunchtime she retreated to the backyard to see if siestas were all they were cracked up to be.

Maybe a life of leisure wasn't that difficult, after all. Stretched out beneath a weeping willow tree with a pitcher of lemonade, Maggie had nothing on her schedule except a long bath later and dinner with John.

She closed her eyes, letting the sultry summer breeze drift across her body, and was about to drift off into sleep when she heard her name. These people were professionals. Why were they asking her opinion? She just owned the place.

"Whatever you want," she mumbled. "Whatever you choose will be all right with me."

"Terrific," came a deep male voice. "Don't say I didn't warn you."

Before she could react, she found herself kissed—and soundly.

Her eyes flew open. "John!" She forced her voice down into its normal register. "What are you doing here?" Didn't successful businessmen have more important things to do than pay unexpected visits?

He glanced toward the house as the sound of hammering floated across the yard to them. "I was on my way to a meeting, and I happened to be going past here." His gaze strayed toward the mob in the parking lot. "Quite a crowd you've got, Maggie."

She smiled blandly and said nothing. What she wanted to do was blindfold him and lead him back to his Jaguar, but the man was curious enough already.

"Is something wrong?" he persisted.

"Of course not," she said, her throat dry. One day into the preparations for the Summit Meeting, and already she'd been found out. Alistair would kill her. "Why on earth would you think that?"

Two electricians and a trio of plumbers strolled past them, lugging masses of equipment.

"Oh, I don't know," John said, scraping his hair off his forehead. "Call it my keen business intuition."

"I'm having some repairs done."

"Repairs? Did a bomb drop on this place?"

He was right. She had enough workmen there to rebuild half of Philadelphia. "If you must know, I'm renovating."

He laughed. "You're kidding!"

His words made her hackles rise. "No, I'm not kidding." And, thanks to careful wording, neither was she lying. "It's something I've planned for a long time."

His golden eyes were sharp as he watched her rise from the chaise. "I thought you had some financial difficulties."

"You think entirely too much, John." She grabbed his hand and marched him back toward the parking lot. "It's very nice of you to drop by, but I'd hate to see you miss your appointment."

He stopped halfway between the main building and his Jaguar. "Don't worry about my appointment. It's only my accountant. Believe me, he'll wait."

She put her hands on his shoulders and pushed him toward his car. "Goodbye, John. I'll see you tonight."

"I want to see what renovations you're doing." His eyes twinkled in the sunlight. "Any heart-shaped bathtubs?"

"Forget it. You're not going to see anything." If he got one glimpse of the sophisticated computer equipment being installed on the first floor, it would be all over. "I'll meet you at seven for dinner."

"I'll pick you up."

"Oh, no, you won't. From now on, The White Elephant is off-limits."

"Even if I promise not to steal your ideas?"

She had to laugh at the studiedly innocent expression on his face. "Even if you sign it in blood. This is business, Tyler."

"When do I get to see the finished product?"

She nudged him into his car. ''In a few weeks.''

*On the front page of every major newspaper in the world.*

She stood in the driveway, and it wasn't until the Jaguar disappeared around the bend that her hands began to shake.

PAX knew how to play rough, and when it came time to secure the grounds for a Summit Meeting, she didn't dare think about what would happen to an intruder.

John couldn't get that close again.

She would have to make certain of that.

WHY HAD HE DONE IT?

John stared at the disaster that used to be Hideaway Haven's legendary nightclub. Empty bottles of Bud Lite glittered in the spotlight. Half-eaten pastrami sandwiches vied for table space with hunks of prime rib worthy of Henry VIII. Slices of pickle and jars of mustard sat forgotten on the steps next to the three exhausted musicians who just happened to be his old friends.

''I must be nuts,'' he said, picking his way over the wires covering the path to the stage. ''I could've said no.'' He pushed aside a faded dill pickle and sat down on the top step, stage right. ''Is it too late to back out?''

Terry, who was sprawled on the floor near the drums, lifted his head. ''Try it and you're dead, Animal. Five days and counting.''

John still wasn't used to hearing his old nickname again, even though for the past ten days it seemed he'd heard little else. Juggling corporate duties with rock 'n' roll had him feeling slightly schizophrenic.

''How the hell did I get that name anyway?'' he asked, eyeing a pickle spear with suspicion.

Frankie laughed from his perch under a speaker. "The way I remember it, it was that time you..." He recounted an incident in San Diego that made John blanch.

"Yeah, I think I remember now."

Sometimes it amazed him that he'd made it to thirty-five with all of his body parts still attached. "I'm not rehearsing again tonight, guys."

"So what else is new?" Terry stifled a yawn. "You been skipping out on us every night since we got here."

John listed a fraction of his corporate holdings. "These things take time."

"Yeah, and so do beautiful women."

"Can't argue with that," said John, thinking of Maggie and the last nine evenings he'd spent with her. They'd dined at every great restaurant between there and Delaware, including Le Bec Fin and were sated on great wine and greater food, soft candlelight and sweet music.

All the elements for a great romance were there for the asking.

Except one.

For two adults who between them owned three hundred and seventeen bedrooms, they were incredibly reluctant to do their romancing anywhere but the front seat of his car.

But there was no way around it.

With his three pals staying in the main house and the No Vacancy sign posted, there was no way John could invite Maggie in.

You didn't bed your future wife with your middle-aged high school buddies snickering down on the ground floor.

And Maggie had told him in no uncertain terms that The White Elephant was off-limits at the moment. Every time he so much as suggested picking her up at the inn, she reminded him that he was her competition and she wasn't about to let him in on any of her secrets.

The morning he'd dropped in on her unexpectedly she'd seemed nervous and uncomfortable, more so than the situation had warranted.

But, then, his vantage point was vastly different than hers. Hideaway Haven was just part of his empire. In a year or two business would be stabilized, and he would move on to another challenge.

The White Elephant was everything to Maggie.

She'd made it clear the inn was out of bounds until the renovations were completed, and for now he would respect her wishes.

Unfortunately so were every other hotel, motel and inn in the area. The last thing either one of them needed was another front-page picture in the *Pocono Bugle* and a cute story about "love in the air."

So for nine nights he'd tortured himself with wild bouts of necking in his Jaguar that left him wired and ready to snap.

Something had to give, and soon, or he wouldn't be held responsible for his actions.

"Is there something wrong with your hearing, Animal?"

John started, knocking a pickle spear down onto the red plush carpeting that outlined the dance floor. "Did I miss something?"

Terry shook his head, amused. "You're really out of it, guy. Better get some sleep tonight."

John waited for the bawdy remark. "I'm disappointed," he said after a moment. "I figured there was a punch line to that statement."

Terry laughed and cadged a cigarette from Frankie. "No punch line. We just decided to check out some of the local establishments before the wives show up tomorrow. Maybe sit in with a couple of bands.''

"Great idea," said John, imagining how the Pennsy Polka Princes would feel about jamming with three leather-jacketed types from Brooklyn. "Have fun."

Terry lowered his voice. "We'll be out most of the night."

He scratched his head in amazement. "I'm slipping, aren't I?"

"Damned straight. I thought you exec types jump to the bottom line right off the bat."

"Getting old," he said. "Don't see the obvious anymore." He thought of Maggie. "How late did you say you'd be out?"

Terry shrugged. "One, maybe two."

John grinned. "Enjoy yourself."

"You, too." To his complete amazement, Terry managed to keep a straight face.

The fire had already been lit.

Tonight it was time to fan the flames.

NINE EVENINGS OF breathless, glorious kissing—and little else—were making a wreck out of Maggie.

Where was the intrepid spirit of the hopeless romantic?

There was no reason on earth Maggie could determine that explained John's not asking her in for coffee. Or drinks. Or a grand tour of that unique room on the third floor.

Perhaps John had her pegged as a cautious, careful woman, the kind of woman who needed a slow and thorough wooing.

Well, that slow and thorough wooing was doing Maggie in.

Those lingering kisses on the dance floor of Andre's, the banquette of Le Petit and the front seat of his Jaguar were making her crazy.

So was the feel of his fingers against the small of her back. And the way his back muscles rippled beneath his dress shirt as she ran her palms across his massive shoulders.

Nine evenings of driving home in a sensual fog more powerful than anything champagne could induce.

Nine evenings of lying awake, looking at her freshly painted ceiling, wondering when on earth John was going to make his move.

Finally on the tenth night, when the windows on the Jaguar fogged after their first kiss, he invited her inside.

They strolled casually into the sun room, each trying to pretend that there was nothing out of the ordinary about it.

He poured them each a snifter of brandy.

They picked up where they'd left off in the car, necking and talking in the way that was becoming as familiar to Maggie as the sound of her own breathing.

"So, what next? You graduated Antioch and—"

Maggie tilted her head slightly left as John nibbled along the side of her neck. "I traveled. I worked. I got married." She slipped her hands inside the open neck of his shirt, hoping to throw a distraction in his path. "Nothing too exciting."

"Where'd you go—Tahiti? The Marquesas?"

She shivered with pleasure as he gently tugged her earlobe. "The usual early seventies' itinerary: bummed my way around Europe." *With a Rolls-Royce and expense account and access to the same information as the president and the premier.*

He stretched full-length on the sofa and drew Maggie down on top of him. "I find it hard to believe you've ever done anything ordinary, Maggie. It just doesn't fit the image."

"Image?" She laughed against his shoulder. "I didn't know I had one."

"You've got one, all right." His fingers massaged the base of her spine, and she felt as hedonistic as a kitten stretching in a pool of sunshine. "The mystery woman."

The muscles in her shoulders stiffened, and she hoped he wouldn't notice. "Should I call my lawyers?" she asked lightly.

"Depends on how you feel about being mysterious. It seems you've kept a pretty low profile around here the last few years."

"That shouldn't be so hard to understand. I did lose my husband, John."

He massaged his way up to her shoulders, obviously aware of the tension gathering there. "Rumor has it you've struck out more men than Gooden and Guidry combined."

For a moment there she'd been afraid her PAX connections might be coming back to haunt her, but she should have known better. The organization had covered her tracks so smoothly that not even Rick had ever known about his wife the spy.

"I have high standards," she said, kissing his delectable lower lip. "Few men can live up to them."

"Is that a challenge?" He turned on his side, wedging her between his hard body and the soft couch.

"Think you're up to one?" It was a dangerous question, but then it had been a long time since she'd found danger so irresistible.

"Try me, Maggie."

His right leg gently imprisoned her as he pressed her deeper into the cushions. She felt as if she were floating somewhere above the clouds with John's strong, demanding body her only anchor to the earth below.

His right hand rested against the base of her throat, then inch by agonizing inch, he brought his fingers down until her breast filled his hand. She might as well have been naked against him because the thin silk shirt she wore was little protection against the fire of his touch.

How could she have lived so long without understanding something so basic?

Something so wonderful and magical and all-encompassing that she had drifted back to The White Elephant each night painfully, gloriously alive in every pore, every cell, every fiber of her body.

He broke the kiss abruptly and, with his eyes meeting hers, swiftly unbuttoned her blouse. The cool breeze on her heated skin made her gasp.

''Take my shirt off,'' he ordered.

Her fingers trembled at the buttons, then slid the soft cotton over his shoulders and down his arms until his chest was bare.

She'd noticed the tan and the muscles that first afternoon at the Bronze Penguin, so the fact that he was beautifully made should have come as no surprise.

Yet how different it all was here in this quiet room with no one to see them.

He'd been defenseless at the Bronze Penguin.

He was anything but defenseless tonight.

She pressed her cheek against him as she had the first time, listened to the acceleration of his heart and gloried that she was the reason for it.

Had this marvelous power always been hers?

She brushed feathery kisses over the curling hair of his chest, then circled the tip of her tongue around his flat dark nipple. His hand rested atop her head, caressing her scalp, and she took his nipple into her mouth, delighting in the texture and taste of his skin.

He said something quietly, matter-of-factly. Something that needed to be said in dangerous times such as these.

She laughed softly, immensely pleased. "That's the most romantic thing anyone ever said to me, John."

"Give me your hand, Maggie."

She looked up at him, letting her hair trail across his bare chest, and did as he asked.

He covered her hand with his and, as her heart beat fiercely against her ribs, guided her until her hand rested against the hardness straining for release.

Her fingers curved to hold him. The heat from his body burned through the layers of fabric separating them.

"I wanted you to know." His voice was low, demanding.

Her eyes fluttered shut against the images, erotic and wonderful, rising before her. "It's the same for me."

The sexually charged sizzle in the room grew stronger, more compelling. It was going to happen.

It had to happen.

It was impossible to have so much emotion flooding your body and not express it the way it should be expressed.

"John..." His name was almost a moan. "I—"

He stopped kissing the curve of her breast and raised his head. "Did you hear something?"

Maggie was beyond hearing anything but the sound of their hearts pounding.

"Damn it!" He raised himself to a sitting position. "I told security the house would be empty."

He rebuttoned her blouse and slipped his shirt back on.

She caught herself wondering how many times in her life she would see him perform that same ritual and realized she had spiraled headfirst into a crazy kind of courtship that was progressing faster than the speed of light.

"I'll be back." He stood up and tucked his shirttail into his pants. "Then we should think about moving upstairs."

To the Garden of Eden on the third floor?

She didn't know if she was ready for that.

"Maybe we should save that room for some other night," she managed.

He grinned and kissed the top of her head while she lounged back against the sofa cushions. "I meant my apartment, Maggie. I'll be right back."

Shamelessly she ogled him as he walked out of the room, delighting in the juxtaposition of wide shoulders and lean hips, wondering how it would be when the time finally came.

"Wonderful," she said aloud, with a shrug. She knew darned well how it would be.

Everything about John was wonderful.

He was opinionated and bright and perceptive, and if she'd been asked to describe the perfect man all she'd need do was dig up a résumé and an eight-by-ten glossy of John Adams Tyler.

He plied her with sinful dinners and sweet music. He tantalized her with brandy so full-bodied it was almost obscene.

But more than that, he captivated her imagination.

He told her stories about his childhood in Brooklyn that made her wish she'd had a chance to play ball against a stoop or go to Tee's for a chocolate egg cream. He told her about the woman he'd loved years ago and how he'd let everything on earth get between them.

They talked about their childhoods—uncomplicated—their families—normal—and their goals—happiness followed by success.

He spread his life out before her, both the dark and the light, and she knew that the dossier she'd left unread couldn't begin to capture the man he really was.

Tonight she would have gone to bed with him. Her mind and her heart and her body yearned for him in a way she'd never imagined. If he'd kissed her one more time she would have followed him up the stairs to that ridiculous water bed and given herself to him gladly.

But he wanted more.

He wanted a commitment she couldn't make.

At least, not yet.

For the next two weeks there were secrets she'd sworn to keep and promises she couldn't break.

It was bad enough she could never tell him about her past life with PAX. Explaining the hundreds of workers swarming over The White Elephant at that very moment would be impossible.

How could he understand something she couldn't explain?

She rose from the couch and straightened the collar of her blouse. Her skirt had risen high above her knees, and she gave it a sharp tug to put it back in place. Many more nights feasting on chateaubriand and lobster and this skirt would be a thing of the past.

Actually, elastic waistbands were beginning to sound quite appealing. . . .

She strolled around the sun room, looking out at the moon shimmering over the lake beyond the French doors, checking for maker's marks on the antique sideboard near the bar.

The clock on the mantel tolled the hour.

What on earth was John doing?

The kitchen was right down the hall. Checking on a noise shouldn't take that long.

She headed down the hallway. There was nothing like restrained sexuality to get your adrenaline pumping.

She swung open the door and stopped dead.

The disreputable group of motorcycle maniacs she'd seen that first night were seated at John's kitchen table about to dig into three pizzas and two six-packs.

The blond guy she'd knocked flat raised his hands in the air. "I'm unarmed," he said, only half-kidding. "You don't have to deck me again."

"Don't worry," she said quickly, her mind elsewhere. "I've taken a vow of pacifism."

There leaning against the refrigerator with his hands in his pockets was John.

"I've taken a vow of celibacy," he mumbled as she walked over to him.

"I don't believe this! What are they doing here?"

"Beats hell out of me. They were supposed to be out painting the town."

"Small town," said the man with the curly red hair. "Only took one coat."

She thought about what had been going on, on that couch in the sun room. Her knees buckled, and she leaned against the refrigerator next to John. "That was a close call."

He made a sound that was a cross between laughter and disgust. "Tell me about it."

She rested her head against his shoulder and sighed. "What are we going to do?"

The red-haired man looked up at them and grinned. "Pizza, anyone?"

John murmured something under his breath about ax murders, and she laughed out loud.

"Speak for yourself, John," she said, taking a seat at the table. "I've always favored poison." She glanced at the name of the pizzeria on the box. "Alfonso's," she said with a nod. "He owed me a favor."

The three men stopped, pizza halfway to their mouths, and stared at her. She smiled sweetly. "*Bon appétit,* boys."

## Chapter Fourteen

Holland might as well have been eating pepperoni pizza for all the pleasure she was getting out of her meal. Caviar and blini and beef Stroganoff—Alistair was wasting his money.

Nothing, even dinner at the Russian Tea Room, could change the way she felt.

She pushed back her chair and rose. "Excuse me," she said, then turned to head for the staircase up to the ladies' room.

"I'd better go with her," she heard Joanna say to Ryder and Alistair. "Order dessert."

"We're not nuns," Holland said over her shoulder as she stalked through the restaurant. "We don't have to travel in pairs."

Joanna restrained herself admirably as they negotiated the staircase, but the bathroom door had barely swung closed before she grabbed the rope of pearls around Holland's neck.

"Those are real, Jo," Holland murmured, extricating herself from her friend's grasp. "Thirty-six inches, perfectly matched. A birthday gift *to* me *from* me." She unsnapped her bracelet and tossed it at Joanna. "If you must break something, amuse yourself with costume."

Joanna took the bracelet and spiked it to the marble floor. Holland watched as it rolled under an unoccupied stall.

"So it's going to be one of those conversations, is it?"

"What on earth is going on?" Joanna tugged again at the pearls as if she wanted to strangle Holland with them. "I know all about getting caught up in your role, but this ice-bitch act is wearing thin."

"Act?" Holland settled herself down at the vanity and inspected her eye makeup in the mirror. "What act?" *You deserve an Emmy, old girl.*

Joanna grabbed her shoulders and spun her around. "Look at me, dammit! I want to know why you're on this self-destruct mission with Alistair."

"Marriage must agree with you, darling," Holland purred. "You're becoming downright dictatorial."

It had also made her extremely single-minded.

"I thought you loved him," Joanna persisted. "I thought everything was wonderful."

"You think way too much." Holland opened her purse and extracted a cigarette. "Do you have a match?"

"I don't smoke." Joanna grabbed her wrist and looked at the cigarette. "Virginia Slims? Since when? I thought you'd been converted to Gauloise?"

"Where's your patriotism?" Holland snapped, tossing the unlit cigarette down on the vanity. "Buy American, and all that."

Joanna perched on the edge of the vanity. "Does that policy extend to your personal life, too?"

Holland lowered her head and rested her face in her hands. "Don't, Jo. I'm not in the mood. Back off."

"I can't back off. I've known you too long to back off."

"This is difficult enough. I don't need your unsolicited opinion."

Joanna gave her a sharp kick.

"Careful, darling," Holland said, rubbing her ankle. "You're abusing the highest paid actress on daytime television."

"You're lucky I don't give you a black eye." She grabbed Holland by the lapels of her Chinese silk smoking jacket. "Why are you doing it? Have you gone crazy?"

"None of your business."

"It is my business. If it hadn't been for Ryder and me, you never would have met Alistair."

"Correction: our elegant Mr. Chambers picked me up in the lobby of your apartment building. You, as I recall, had nothing whatsoever to do with it."

"Ungrateful wretch. If you hadn't been sitting in the lobby waiting for me, you'd never have been picked up in the first place."

Holland called up her best Act III, Scene IV glare. "At the moment that's hardly a recommendation, Joanna."

"Please," Joanna said, touching her arm, "I know all about privacy and everything else, but I'm worried, Holland. What's going on?"

That touch was Holland's undoing.

She lay her head down on her arms and started to cry.

"YOU'VE LOOKED at your watch three times in the last ten minutes," Alistair said to Ryder as they polished off their brandy.

The younger man glanced toward the doorway and then back. "They've been gone a hell of a long time, Chambers."

Alistair shrugged. "Talking about us, no doubt."

Ryder chuckled. "Talking about you is more like it. The atmosphere in this room has been a little cold this evening, wouldn't you say?"

"Things went well," Alistair said, careful to keep his tone even.

Ryder laughed out loud. "Things went well? If they went any worse, she would have stabbed you with the butter knife."

"Holland is under stress at work."

"Holland is mad as hell at you."

"As usual, you exaggerate."

Ryder glared at him. "As usual you see what you want to see. Joanna told me Holland is running out of patience."

Alistair offered his friend a cigarette and, after Ryder refused, drew one out of the packet for himself. "I see a man who is overstepping the bounds of propriety."

"Screw propriety!"

"Charming," Alistair muttered. "So eloquent."

"You're losing her, Chambers, and you don't seem to give a damn."

Alistair lit his Gauloise and inhaled deeply. "Things are under control."

Ryder slammed his hand down on the tabletop, drawing a snort of disapproval from the headwaiter across the room.

"Careful, my boy," Alistair said. "When one is given a booth at the Tea Room, one is expected to behave with decorum."

"You can take your decorum and shove it."

"Aren't you a bit old for this Young Turk routine, Ryder?"

"And aren't you a bit old for this loner routine?" Ryder countered.

"As I said, things are under control."

"Not from where I sit."

Alistair ignored him. "How are things progressing on the Steel project?"

"He leaves for Hawaii next month for stage two. Chambers, I—"

"And Madison is still scheduled to vacation there?"

"Yes, dammit! We can talk business later. I want to know what you're going to do about Holland."

"None of your business, Ryder." Alistair exhaled, letting the plume of fragrant smoke drift across the table.

"I'm your friend, Chambers. I don't want to see you piss away your last chance for happiness."

"May I quote you on that?"

"You can do any damn thing you want as long as you answer me."

A waiter swooped down on their table with a fresh ashtray. Alistair nodded his thanks and rested his cigarette on the edge. "Although this is none of your business and I highly resent being put in the position of defending my behavior, I shall endeavor to answer your question, anyway." He fixed his friend, protégé and surrogate son with his most authoritative look. "After the Summit Meeting, I intend to ask Holland to marry me."

Ryder stared at him as if he'd announced his intentions to propose to the Queen of England.

"Any objections?"

"I can't believe it. How many times did you tell me that marriage and the organization were incompatible?" He raked his unruly hair off his forehead with a sharp, impatient gesture. "Damn it, Alistair! You were right about all that. If Joanna weren't in PAX, I don't know how in hell I'd explain the trips and the phone calls and the roomfuls of equipment. Holland is a bright woman. She has a high profile. How in hell could you ever—'' He stopped. "You're not."

Alistair grinned. "I am."

"Not you."

"Afraid so."

"You're an institution."

"Institutions get lonely."

Ryder leaned back in his seat and, after a long moment, he threw back his head and laughed. "Well, hot damn! Alistair Chambers is going to retire."

"I NEVER CRY," Holland said as she repaired her mascara. She looked at Joanna in the mirror and forced a smile. "That is, I never cry unless *Destiny* is paying me for it."

Joanna, who had shed a few tears herself, snapped the lid back on her eye shadow and met Holland's gaze. "I wish I knew what to say to you, Holland. Fine friend I am. You tell me you're breaking up with Alistair, and I start to cry." She shook her head angrily. "Who would have figured it?"

"Yeah," said Holland, recapping her mascara. "Ironic, isn't it? All those years I said I'd give everything up if the right man came along, and now that the right man has come along I find I don't want to give everything up." She ran a brush through her hair and tossed it into her purse. "Not that any man has asked me to give anything up, you understand."

Joanna started to say something before she apparently thought better of it.

"Look," said Holland, suddenly exhausted, "I know there are things I'm not supposed to wonder about, things that you understand." Joanna's mouth opened in protest, but Holland raised her hand. "I'm not going to ask any questions. I simply can't live on the outside any longer."

"It's because he's leaving next week, isn't it?"

Holland shrugged. "Let's just say that was the last straw in a long series of last straws. Do you realize how many times I humiliated myself talking about marriage and commitment with a man who's married to something I don't understand?" She slipped her bracelet back on. "Coming in second is bad enough, Jo, but not knowing what's coming in first is even worse. I deserve better."

"Talk to him about it," Joanna urged as they stood up and got ready to return to the main dining room. "Don't do something you'll regret."

But Holland knew it had gone too far for that.

She knew she'd regret it for the rest of her life.

JOHN AND MAGGIE were sitting on the back steps listening to the sound of the crickets and the summer wind rustling though the trees. The sky was clear and lit with stars, and it would have been a wonderful night for love.

"Out in the cold again," he said, stroking her hair gently. "I can't believe it." It was a good thing this wasn't a winter courtship.

"Neither can I." Maggie laced her fingers with his. "You should have told me you had houseguests, John."

"They were supposed to be out painting the town, remember?"

Maggie sighed deeply as he pulled her closer against his body. "I've been wondering why you haven't asked me in for coffee."

"Now you know," he said, smiling into the darkness. "Who the hell would want to sit around watching those guys tune their guitars?"

"I like those guys. They're your friends."

"Not much of a recommendation, Maggie." He paused. "You like them?"

"They told me all your deep, dark secrets. What's not to like?"

"I have to have a long talk with them."

"Why didn't you tell me you guys were famous?"

"I told you we used to sing together."

"Yes, John, but you didn't tell me you were The Domino Theory. I bet I have one of your old albums stashed away somewhere."

He laughed. "I doubt that, Maggie. At first you thought The Domino Theory was a political activist group."

"What can I say? I spent a lot of my time out of this country back then." She brushed a strand of her hair off his face. "Were you really going to keep that concert at the Garden a secret?"

"You got it."

"I don't understand."

"I never really liked performing. I didn't get anything out of standing up there on stage waiting for applause."

"Then why are you doing this show?."

"I owe it to them," he said, gesturing back toward the house. "I walked out on the group pretty suddenly. They deserved better."

Like this second chance at success.

"I'm dying to see you onstage." She snuggled closer to him. "I love leather jackets, John."

"I can't believe it. I've been wasting my time with the three-piece suits and the five-star restaurants."

"Well, let's not get crazy. I love five-star restaurants."

He moved away until he could see her face in the moonlight. "You'll come to the Garden?"

She placed a kiss against his jaw. "Try and stop me."

Heat, fierce and sudden, spread throughout his body. "I have a suite reserved at the Plaza, Maggie."

The look she gave him was powerful. "With a view of the Park?"

"With a view of the Park."

She linked her hands behind his neck. "Is that an invitation, Mr. Tyler?"

"Yes," he said, bringing his mouth toward hers.

"Yes," she whispered against his lips. "Yes, yes, yes."

*Sorry, guys,* he thought, *but you're being bumped to the Waldorf.*

ALISTAIR SAT in the wing chair listening quietly as the woman he loved told him it was over.

Decades of training made it possible for him to maintain a stoic calm on the outside, while inside he railed to the heavens at this bloody example of bad timing.

Holland was standing at the window, her lovely face silhouetted against the ivory curtains. "No explanation?" she said, her voice quiet and controlled. "No last minute pardon from the governor?"

"None," he said, cursing PAX and the Summit Meeting and a world that made Summit Meetings necessary. "If it were up to me, my love, I would—"

She raised an elegant hand in protest. "Don't," she whispered. "There's no point to it. It's taken me forty-four years to get here, and I may lose my nerve."

"I don't understand."

"No, I don't suppose you would. You've never had to choose, have you, darling?"

That fine female arrogance that covered her very human heart.

How little she knew.

How he wished he could tell her he was about to make the first choice of his life.

Instead he pulled her into his arms before he turned and walked out the door.

In ten days it would be over, and he would be able to ask her.

In ten days, God willing, she would say yes.

MAGGIE GLARED at her uncle across the table at The White Elephant four days later.

"What do you mean you're moving up the date, Alistair? I thought things were already set in motion."

"Best laid plans, et cetera et cetera. You of all people should understand that." He pushed aside a maze of wires and dug out an ashtray. "Actually this was part of the original plan."

Maggie yanked the ashtray out of his hand and tossed it into the trash bin near the swinging door. "You should have told me."

"I didn't dare, my girl. You aren't as circumspect as one would like."

"I have plans for that night, Alistair." She thought about the Plaza and the suite with the view of the Park. "I can't leave for Bermuda for at least another day or two."

"Not good enough, Magdalena. We need you secured before that."

She wrinkled her nose. "You make me sound like a piece of furniture."

"Would that you were so easy to contain." He found another ashtray. "Sensibilities have no place in this business. That much I thought you remembered."

"That much I've been trying to forget. If you recall, I'm not in this business any longer."

"Afraid you are, my girl." He lit a cigarette, ignoring her furious glare. "At least for the next ten days."

"I refuse to change my plans."

"Don't worry," he said, letting the smoke out slowly. "You can still see The Domino Theory at the Garden on Thursday."

She felt her jaw slack open. "How in God's name do you know about that?"

"Trade secret."

"I resent having my privacy invaded."

"Then you shouldn't have agreed to my offer, Magdalena. This comes with territory."

"So Big Brother's still watching," she mumbled. "What else do you know, Ally?"

To her amazement, her uncle's aristocratic face reddened. "A great deal."

"Don't tell me you know about the Plaza?"

He nodded. "Mr. Tyler has excellent connections, my girl. The view of the Park from that suite is unparalleled."

She jumped up from her seat, toppling the chair onto the tiled floor with a crash. "I can't believe it! You probably have the room bugged."

"I'm wounded," said Alistair. "PAX holds young lovers in the highest esteem."

"We're not lovers."

"Be that as it may, we would never infringe upon your privacy."

"Easy for you to say now," she countered. "I won't even be in that room for you to infringe upon anything."

"Sailing off to Bermuda on *La Jolie* is scarcely a life sentence at hard labor."

"No," she said. "It's more like solitary confinement."

He stubbed out his cigarette. "You'd like to invite your beau."

What a wonderfully old-fashioned word.

Maggie nodded. "It seems the wisest course of action, Alistair." A grin tugged at her mouth. "You certainly don't want him poking around the premises here, do you?"

Her uncle's bright blue eyes twinkled with amusement. "We certainly don't."

"If he's in Bermuda, you won't have to worry."

"Your concern overwhelms me, my girl."

"It's either that or the Plaza, Ally. Take your pick."

He threw his head back and laughed loud and long. "Sometimes I forget how like your Aunt Sarah you are."

"Aunt Sarah issued ultimatums, too?"

He stopped laughing and met her eyes. "She knew how to get around me, same as you."

"Does that mean yes to Bermuda?"

"That means yes to Bermuda." He laid out the ground rules, and Maggie listened intently. "He's a smart man, Maggie. You'll need a good cover story to explain this trip."

She snapped her fingers. "I'll simply tell John I have a generous uncle."

Bermuda.

Pink sands.

Gentle waters.

Sunsets seen from the deck of a private yacht.

John.

She shivered as a wave of longing washed over her.

"Don't worry about a thing, Ally," she said. "From here on in, it's going to be clear sailing."

# Chapter Fifteen

"Cut. Enjoy your weekend, boys and girls."

Holland put the Baccarat wineglass down on the end table and headed for her dressing room.

"Good work, Holland," the director said as she passed him in the doorway. "You really nailed Caroline's fury over Jason's defection. Who says the method doesn't work?"

Holland flashed him her best smile. "The Method," she said. "Where would we be without it?"

*Fool!*

Who needed the Method when you had a bona fide broken heart to draw on for inspiration?

Idiotic tears stung at her eyes as she hurried to the privacy of her dressing room.

Why on earth had she ever thought breaking up with Alistair was the right thing to do?

She'd expected an argument from him, a fine rage, harsh words spoken in the heat of anger and passion.

At the very least she'd expected him to storm out of her apartment, slamming the door behind him.

She got none of that.

Not even in the face of high romantic drama had that bloody British reserve of his failed him.

In fact he didn't even seem to understand that they'd broken up at all. He'd merely kissed her at the door, and two hours later a baker's dozen long-stemmed red roses had arrived in a glossy white box tied with scarlet ribbons.

She sat down in front of her mirror, pushed aside three vases of flowers and began tissuing off the thick layers of Pan-Cake that turned Holland Masters into Caroline, daytime TV's number-one bitch.

Each and every day since the alleged breakup, a dozen roses plus one had arrived at her home, at her dressing room, at her agent's office, all with the same ivory card with the single word: Patience.

"Patience!" She tossed the tissues into the wastebasket next to the dressing table. She'd had nothing but patience for two years, and where had it gotten her?

Nowhere, that's where.

He was still secretive, still mysterious, still as maddeningly out of reach as he'd ever been.

Well, damn it, she didn't need that.

Her entire life had been spread out in front of Alistair like a smorgasbord, and he hadn't offered her anything more substantial than an appetizer.

A tantalizing appetizer she had to admit, but an appetizer nonetheless. She knew there'd been a wife named Sarah whom he loved. She knew there was a niece named Maggie whom he adored. She knew that Ryder and Joanna were closer to him than almost anyone on earth.

So what?

What were his dreams?

What was it that beckoned when he left her suddenly in the middle of the night?

Where did he go, and what did he do once he got there?

And the biggest question of all: If it really was over, why on earth did she still care?

"Love?" She tossed a makeup sponge at her reflection. "Bah, humbug!"

BERMUDA.

John stared up at the ceiling. He'd tried counting sheep, stock options and bank accounts, but no dice.

If he had any brains he'd be asleep by now. Tomorrow night was the big concert at the Garden, and for the next forty-eight hours he knew he'd be running on caffeine and adrenaline.

Eight hours' sleep would be a nice cushion between him and exhaustion.

But Maggie's surprising offer had him wide awake.

There was a hell of a big difference between a suite at the Plaza and a yacht off Bermuda, even if said yacht did belong to her uncle.

The Maggie he knew was more comfortable in jeans than designer dresses.

A suite at the Plaza had seemed to impress her.

At least that's what he'd thought before he discovered there was a seventy-foot yacht awaiting her arrival.

John was a New Yorker at heart, and he'd liked the idea of their first time together being in the city he loved.

A ride through the Park in a hansom cab. Dinner at Tavern on the Green with the white lights twinkling in the trees. The Plaza, with a hundred years of romantic tradition lurking behind every settee and marble column.

Where better to officially propose to the woman he intended to marry?

He'd done his damnedest to convince her of the wonders of the Big Apple, but she wouldn't give an inch, not even to consider one night in Manhattan followed by four nights on the high seas.

John punched his pillow and turned over. Why hadn't he noticed before exactly how stubborn Maggie was?

Every now and then he became aware of an almost palpable barrier around her, an invisible shield that seemed to be keeping him an arm's length away from ever understanding exactly what she was all about.

Bermuda.

He couldn't help wondering if there was more to the lure of the island than simply what met the eye.

Pink sandy beaches.

Gentle breezes.

A seventy-foot yacht, complete with crew.

No telephones, no newspapers, no interruptions.

Nothing but the open sea and Maggie in a bikini.

Maybe they could go to the Plaza on their wedding night instead.

HER BAGS WERE PACKED, and the limousine John had sent was waiting in the driveway. All Maggie had to do was get her last-minute instructions from Alistair and she was off to Madison Square Garden. And Bermuda.

She found him in the drawing room, hidden behind a mainframe computer the size of her floor-to-ceiling bookcases.

"Well," she said, posing in the doorway. "I'm ready to go."

He looked up. "Maggie?"

She flicked her teased, moussed and ruthlessly straightened hair over her shoulder. "Am I groovy or what?"

"Good God in heaven! Is that you?"

"Yes, it is," she said, laughing. "Maggie Douglass, circa 1969."

Her uncle's eyes lingered on her shiny white go-go boots, skipped quickly up her fishnet-stockinged legs, darted over her leather mini and black poor boy sweater, then stopped dead on her face.

"I have never seen so much eye makeup on another living woman."

"This was called the natural look back then."

He muttered something and shook his head. "Incredible. American ingenuity."

"Oh, don't blame us! Back in the sixties all of our styles were set on Carnaby Street." Makeup was from Yardley of London. Hairstyles by Sassoon. Clothing, thanks to Mary Quant.

"Makes one wonder if the Empire is in deep trouble," he said.

"Be objective, Ally." She pirouetted. "What do you think?"

He looked as if Harrod's window had blown up on his doorstep. "You look like a tart."

"You old darling! You always know the right thing to say." She kissed his cheek. "Do you have the tickets and everything for me?"

He pulled a suede pouch out of the briefcase he kept next to him at all times. "Ready and waiting. You have time for exactly one glass of champagne after the concert, then it's off to the airport."

Alistair was apologetic over the fact they weren't flying first-class.

"I understand," she said, tucking the tickets away. "It was short notice, and we couldn't very well take the PAX jet, could we?"

"No, my girl, you could not." His voiced softened. "Have a grand time."

She tried to thank him, but her voice momentarily faltered. "I don't know what to say, Ally. I—" she cleared her throat "—you've done so much." The White Elephant was now a model of turn-of-the-century charm and splendor. After the Summit Meeting was over this weekend, success was a sure thing.

She'd waited so long for it that now that the moment was here, she found it hard to believe. "I feel like Cinderella with the clock about to strike midnight." She peered out the window at the stretch limo in the driveway. "Some pumpkin."

"I think your imagination is running away with you, Maggie, but that's understandable. Love does those things."

She could feel the heat building in her cheeks, but she made no motion to hide the fact. "I've been that obvious?"

"Classic symptoms. I recognized them immediately."

"I can't thank you enough, Alistair, for all you've done. You made all my dreams for The White Elephant come true."

"You would have made them all come true on your own. PAX just gave them an added push in the right direction."

"And this won't all disappear when the clock strikes midnight?"

He laughed and walked her to the front door. "Just make certain that when it does strike midnight, you and your Mr. Tyler are on a plane bound for Bermuda."

"Don't worry about a thing, Ally. That's one thing you can count on."

THERE WAS SOMETHING to be said for life in the fast lane, Maggie thought, as the limousine whisked into the reserved parking spot.

No sweaty subways.

No crowded buses.

No crazy cabdrivers whose sole English words were "accident," and "Don't make change."

The driver got out and ran around to open her door. She exited to the oohs and aahs of a throng of fans cordoned off just beyond the stage entrance. Scraps of whispered comments about her legs and her hair filtered to her as she strode to the door, but it wasn't until she heard the word groupie that she started to laugh.

Maggie Douglass, groupie.

Less than one month ago she'd been waging a one-woman campaign against tackiness in the Poconos, and now there she was looking like a rock and roll queen.

Where were her values?

Where was her good taste?

She flashed her backstage pass at the guard and stepped into the madhouse.

*What's the matter, Douglass?*

Where was her sense of adventure?

She looked up at a man who sported earrings shaped like green rubber snakes. This was as good a place as any to start.

"Excuse me," she said. "Could you tell me where the—"

"Paul!" A woman in gold spandex who was old enough to be Maggie's grandmother raced up to the snake man. "Deep Six says they won't go on if we don't ship in Perrier pronto. Why don't you—" They disappeared into the crowd of reporters and camera crews milling around the rolling bar.

A friendly photographer from *Newsweek* took a picture of Maggie, then showed her how to thread her way through the backstage tangle and find the seats reserved for guests.

Her seat was front row, center. She shamelessly twisted around, scanning the audience, and easily picked out four Kennedys, Christie Brinkley and her husband, Billy Joel, and more Brat Pack movie stars than she could identify.

The lights went down.

If the applause and cheers from the audience were any indication, the opening acts were good, but Maggie couldn't hear over the violent pounding of her heart.

"And now," the voice from the loudspeaker boomed, "what you've all be waiting for, the group that gave street corners a good name: The Domino Theory!"

The stage went black, and then suddenly an amber spotlight found John.

He looked mean and angry, dangerous and too sexy for words.

He grabbed the microphone, and before the first song was over, Maggie understood what animal magnetism was all about.

THE APPLAUSE RUSHED toward him like a runaway train, and in that moment John knew he had that damned audience in the palm of his hand.

"You nailed 'em," Terry said as they set up the next song. "It's in the bag."

John said nothing.

After all the years and all the changes, standing there in the heat of the spotlight, basking in the applause, he'd almost forgotten why he'd said yes in the first place.

But looking at Terry, he remembered.

This wasn't his world.

It never had been.

It never would be.

The adulation of the faceless crowd wasn't what he wanted or needed. Music wasn't why he got up every morning.

"Animal...Animal...Animal..."

They were beginning to chant that old nickname and, if he let it happen, no one out there would even remember there was anyone else in the group.

He met Terry's eyes. "It's all yours," he said. But then it always was.

He stepped out of the spotlight and made room for the ones who really deserved it.

THE TRANSITION was so smooth, so natural that it took Maggie half a song before she realized what had happened.

From the moment he took the stage she'd seen and heard nothing else.

How could she?

Up there in the spotlight he was pure macho swagger, every fantasy she'd ever had—and a few she hadn't dared.

In those tight faded jeans, the T-shirt, the battered leather jacket, he was the bad boy out to ruin the reputation of every girl in the senior class.

The rest of the group faded next to John.

He looked out over the audience, the conquering warrior surveying the vanquished.

The power was his.

So was the choice.

She understood what he was doing in a way no one else could. Much of her own life had been decided by her own sense of responsibility.

Until that moment, desire had been the ruling force in her relationship with John.

No longer.

When he stepped out of that seductive spotlight and handed the power over to the other men without regret, she knew beyond question that for her there could be no turning back.

"THERE'S NO HOPE for it then." Alistair switched off the computer and rose from behind his desk at Control Center East, aka, The White Elephant. "She'll have to be brought back."

From the leather pouch ever present at his side, he withdrew copies of her travel plans.

"Madison Square Garden?" The tallest of his aides shook his head. "Couldn't do it. Place'll be crawling with photographers. Too risky."

"The airport then," he said, placing his glasses on top of the computer console. "Have her paged and explain the situation."

"What if she gives us trouble?"

"She won't," said Alistair. "She's a professional. She'll do what needs to be done."

He checked his watch, then synchronized it with the others. "Take her car," he said to the men before him. "It will attract less attention. I'll be waiting here."

He wasn't asking her to forego her plans entirely.

He was simply asking her to delay them.

Maggie would understand—she always had before—and once it was over he'd make it up to her with three weeks in Bermuda instead of a few short days.

Foolproof, he thought, lighting a cigarette.

Absolutely foolproof.

Unfortunately Alistair Chambers had forgotten one very important detail: John Adams Tyler, who wouldn't understand anything at all.

## Chapter Sixteen

John slipped into the huge ballroom and watched the party kaleidoscoping around him. Bright streaks of crimson from silk cocktail dresses. Splashes of blue and gold from mock-military uniforms. The sparkle of glitter and the blinding pop of flashbulbs, hot and white.

Fifteen years and not one damned thing had changed.

Bianca and Liza, Cornelia and Jerry—all the media superstars who flocked to concerts the way the faithful flocked to Lourdes.

Old was in, these days. The sixties were hot, and anything and everybody connected with that crazy decade were definitely on the A-list.

College kids clutched The Domino Theory albums, older than they were, to their Benetton chests and asked the same question of everyone over thirty, ''Did you go to Woodstock?''

Fifteen years ago he'd been feeling caged in, ready to move on, praying there'd be more to life than the next gig, wondering if he could make it without his friends and if he was crazy to even try.

Fifteen years ago Maggie Douglass was only a dream, a product of his imagination, the same as the career he wanted to carve.

He drained his bottle of Perrier and spotted her laughing with Terry's wife as the two of them got Cronkite's autograph and headed toward Brinkley, Joel and the Boss.

No sophisticated ennui for Maggie. She was blatantly, unashamedly star struck, and he loved it.

There were no secrets with Maggie, no huge black clouds hovering overhead. She'd grown up in the Midwest, married in the East and buried a husband much too soon. She was ambitious and creative, witty and uncompromisingly honest, and if she sometimes kept a barrier around her emotions—hell, she'd been hurt. That was something he could understand.

Something he could overcome.

She was also sexy as hell in that short leather skirt with her long blond hair flying wild about her shoulders, and if he didn't get her alone within the next eight minutes he'd probably go up in a blaze of protoplasm.

He grinned, the invisible man, as three reporters rushed past him to get to Terry and the guys.

He came up behind Maggie and rested his hand on her hip. "How would you feel about getting out of here for a while, baby?" A bad line, but it was his best preliberation stuff.

She leaned against him for a moment, her face cool and composed. "Depends what you had in mind."

"There's a car outside." His voice was low and intimate, meant for her alone. "We can be at the airport in half an hour."

She considered his words. "Bermuda," she said, looking up at him through her thick, dark false eyelashes. "I'd love to go to Bermuda."

"Your wish is my command."

"And a yacht," she said, her blue eyes sparkling. "There has to be a yacht."

"Shouldn't be a problem."

She made a show of looking at the swarm of reporters surrounding Terry, Frank and Joe. "Think they can get along without you?"

He caught Terry's eye across the room. The red-haired man flashed him a thumbs-up, and John knew they'd never miss him.

"Come on," he said, putting his arm around Maggie's shoulder. "We have a plane to catch."

MAYBE IT WAS THE MOONLIGHT, maybe it was her mood, but the ride from Manhattan to Newark International Airport had never been lovelier.

Even the New Jersey Turnpike seemed blessed with its own magic tonight.

While she'd enjoyed her limousine ride into the city earlier that evening, she adored the ride back out.

And why not?

Wrapped in John's arms, the backseat of her Jeep would seem like paradise.

"You were wonderful tonight," she murmured against his lips. "Absolutely wonderful."

"I'm glad you like my singing," he said, chuckling, "but you told me that already."

"I'm not talking about your singing."

His hand drifted across her stockinged thigh. "What are you talking about, Maggie?"

She moved his hand to a safer, more neutral spot.

"I'm talking about what you did up there on that stage."

He reached over to fiddle with the stereo system, but she turned it off from the master control panel on her door.

"Was it that obvious?" he asked after a moment.

"Not to anyone else." She rested her forehead against his cheek. "That audience belonged to you, John, and you handed them over."

He said nothing, just laced his fingers through hers.

"I hope they appreciate what you did," she said, her voice fierce. "You didn't have to do that."

"Yes, I did." He raised her hand to his mouth and kissed each fingertip. "And it took me fifteen years to get around to it."

It had been a noble act in a business not known for nobility, the act of a man who understood what true generosity was all about.

The act of a man she could spend a lifetime getting to know.

How it had happened that she, a realist of the first order, would find herself in love with a romantic like John was beyond her, but happen it had.

Although she'd fought against it, that same inexplicable malady that he called love at first sight had seized her the moment she saw him walk into the Bronze Penguin.

Beyond the reach of logic and practicality and common sense, her heart had recognized the truth long before her head, and only her promise to Alistair had kept her from throwing herself at John's doorstep and declaring her undying love.

But now she was home free.

She glanced at her watch. In forty-five minutes it would be midnight, and Flight 712, nonstop Newark to Bermuda, would be on its way.

And a few hours later she would be in John's arms.

THEY MADE IT to the airport with no time to spare.

An unexpected traffic jam inside the airport's perimeter had eaten up a chunk of time, and they had less than eight minutes to check in, get their boarding passes and run for the gate.

While Maggie fumbled through her purse looking for the tickets, John coolly reached into her carry-on bag and withdrew the folders.

"Now I know why you're so successful," she said as they raced into the terminal, dragging their luggage behind them. "You're organized."

"Gate 19," said the clerk as she checked their suitcases. "You'd better hurry."

John grabbed Maggie's hand and started to pull her through the empty airport.

"I can't run like that!" she cried, slipping on the freshly waxed tiles. "We'll never make it."

He pointed at her spike-heeled shoes. "If you take those damned things off, we have a fighting chance."

She balanced against him and yanked off her heels. They did a wind sprint down the deserted corridor, whizzed through the security scanning machine, even though the agents looked long and hard at their crazy outfits, and made it to Gate 19 just before Maggie's lungs gave way.

"I see you folks like to live dangerously," said the attendant at the opening to the jet way. "We close the doors in three minutes." He folded John's ticket back, checked the seat number, then reached for Maggie's. "You're Maggie Douglass?"

As if her heart weren't pounding hard enough as it was. "Yes," she managed between gasps. "Is something wrong?'' *Don't tell me PAX can set up a Summit Meeting but can't buy an airline ticket.*

The attendant's smile was bland and noncommittal. "There were three phone calls for you. If you hurry, you can make it to the information desk and back."

"You get settled," John said. "I'll get the messages for you."

"No!" She forced herself to calm down. "I mean, it's probably Alistair—something about our arrangements in Bermuda. You get our seats, and I'll be right back." If the message was from one of the PAX operatives, John would never be able to retrieve it, and she wouldn't know how to answer the inevitable questions.

Before he had a chance to protest, she turned and raced back up the corridor, blessing those long runs through the Pocono countryside for giving her enough stamina to survive this.

"Maggie Douglass," she gasped at the woman behind the information desk. "There's a phone call for me?"

The woman looked up and smiled the same smile as the attendant and the ticket clerk. "Yes, Ms. Douglass. You're a popular lady. Let's see...." She punched in a series of letters on her computer keyboard and hummed unintelligibly while she waited for the file to come up. "This always takes so long. Sometimes I wonder why they don't—"

A man stepped between Maggie and the desk. "Magdalena Douglass?"

Maggie wheeled around to face him. "Yes?"

Two other men joined the first.

"You're to come with us."

Good God, what on earth was happening? She tried to get the information clerk's attention, but she was being flirted with by the youngest of the three football player-sized thugs.

"I'm not going anywhere until I know who you are."

The leader flashed a card she recognized all too well and quickly recited her upper-echelon code number.

"Mr. Chambers asked us to bring you back quickly. There's a Code Blue situation, and your help is needed."

"My help? I can't help anybody. I'm on my way to Bermuda!" What was her uncle thinking? She'd been out of the business for years. Surely there wasn't anything she could do to help them.

"I'm afraid we must ask you to cooperate and accompany us back to East Point. Mr. Chambers will answer all of your questions there."

They tried to usher her out of the airport, but Maggie stood her ground. "I don't think you understand. My plane is about to leave, and someone I care very much about is already on it. I have to go!"

She tried to push past them, but she might as well have tried storming the back field of the Miami Dolphins.

"Ms. Douglass," said the leader, "you're making this unnecessarily difficult."

"Unnecessarily difficult?" Her voice was high and shrill. "You're ruining my life! If I don't make that plane, I'll never be able to explain this to John."

"A moot point," said the leader.

Her stomach lurched. "What do you mean?"

He pointed toward the screen overhead. "Flight 712 has already left for Bermuda." He nodded in approval. "Right on time."

"No!" She broke free and, tossing her high heels to the ground, started to run back toward the gate, but they were too fast for her.

"Mr. Chambers said you might be difficult," the leader said, grabbing her by the waist. "I hate to do this, Ms. Douglass." He whipped out a pair of handcuffs and slapped them on her wrists. "I hope you understand."

Oh, she understood, all right.

She understood that even a hopeless romantic like John would know the brush-off when he saw one.

The pavement scratched the soles of her feet as they hurried her toward the car.

They didn't even have the decency to bring a limousine. Instead they crammed her into the back of her own battered Jeep.

A pumpkin coach would have been better than that.

Some sorry excuse for a Cinderella she was. No glass slippers. No satin gown.

A jet engine roared overhead as she slumped into the back seat.

And Prince Charming on his way nonstop to Bermuda.

"Alistair Chambers," she mumbled as the Jeep lurched out of its parking spot, "I'm going to kill you."

"This is Captain Donnelly. Thank you for choosing Eastern. Temperature at Bermuda Airport is a balmy seventy-eight degrees. Attendants, take your seats and prepare for takeoff."

John grabbed the sleeve of a tall red-haired attendant. "We can't take off!" he blurted. "Maggie—the woman I'm traveling with—isn't on board."

The attendant's eyebrows rushed together in a frown. "She didn't make it to the airport?"

"No, no, she made it to the airport. She had to pick up a message at the information booth. She said she'd be right back, but—"

"Don't worry, sir." She was the epitome of professional calm. "We had a small problem up in first class with some late arrivals. She probably was with the last group and is sitting up there just for takeoff." Her smile widened. "Rules, you understand."

Swiftly she moved up the aisle to claim her own jump seat.

The engines' roar rattled his teeth as the plane gathered speed for takeoff.

She had to be on the plane, he thought as the jet raced down the runway. The information desk was only thirty feet away from Gate 19.

There was no way she could have missed the flight.

The 747 lifted.

*Clunk. Clunk.* The landing gear retracted.

*Ding. Ding.* The no-smoking sign went off.

Son of a bitch. Maggie had missed the plane.

THE FLIGHT ATTENDANTS were terrific.

After an hour of heavy-duty fuming, he finally spoke to some of the crew, and they looked into the other flights from Newark to Bermuda.

There was a good chance Maggie had made a competitor's flight that left thirty-five minutes after this one.

With any luck at all, she would land in Bermuda right around the time he retrieved their baggage.

She didn't.

He sat in the terminal at the Bermuda Airport and waited four and a half hours, and she was a no-show.

No messages. No telegrams. No phone calls. Nothing.

Then it hit him.

Maybe she'd gone straight to the yacht, expecting to meet him there.

So he gathered up all the luggage, dragged everything outside, flagged a taxi and headed for Castle Harbour.

There he was told, in no uncertain terms, that not only was Ms. Magdalena Douglass not on board, she was not expected to be on board.

"Sonesta Beach," he growled to the cabdriver who was unloading the suitcases, "and an extra tip if you don't ask any questions."

The driver arched a dark brow and whistled as he repacked the trunk.

*There's a reason for all of this,* he thought as he crawled beneath the sheets at the hotel. The insane pace he'd been keeping the past two weeks had finally caught up with him, and he was rocky with exhaustion. Right now nothing made any sense.

He'd left messages for Maggie at the airports in both Newark and Bermuda, and with O'Hara at the yacht. He'd even tried calling The White Elephant, but each time, he'd gotten only an earful of static.

When he woke up in the morning there'd be a message from her or a call or, better still, he'd find her curled up beside him.

Yeah, he thought as he closed his eyes. This would all make sense in the morning.

THE TELEPHONE next to the bed jarred him awake a few minutes shy of 6:00 a.m.

"Mr. Tyler?"

"Mmph." He cleared his throat and forced his eyes open. "Speaking."

"This is O'Hara at *La Jolie.*"

"*La Jolie?*"

"Mr. Chambers's yacht."

Suddenly he was wide awake. "You've heard from Ms. Douglass?"

"I most certainly have, sir. You've been cleared to board."

"Ms. Douglass is there?"

"Well, no, sir, she isn't."

"But she's on her way."

"Well, no, sir, she's not."

"She's not there, and she's not on her way there?"

"Correct, sir." The captain's voice brightened. "But we're all ready for you, sir. We have a grand itinerary mapped out for your pleasure."

"But no Ms. Douglass."

"I'm afraid not, sir."

"Thanks," he said, his blood boiling with fury, "but you can tell Ms. Douglass exactly what she can do with her yacht."

A horrified silence from the other end, then, "Sir, perhaps that's a message best delivered in person."

O'Hara was right. John leaped out of bed and grabbed for his clothes. That was exactly what he was going to do.

So he hadn't imagined that invisible barrier around her, that odd little edge of reticence that had intrigued as much as it had puzzled him.

It was there, all right, and he'd run heart first into it.

He wouldn't make that mistake again.

He'd catch the next flight back to the States, and when he got there he'd deliver that message.

And after that, he'd do his damnedest to forget Maggie Douglass ever existed.

# Chapter Seventeen

Maggie's alarm went off at eight the next morning.

She picked up a copy of *Cosmopolitan* from her nightstand and heaved it across the room at the clock.

Bull's-eye.

That was one alarm clock that wouldn't bother an innocent citizen again.

That was more than she could say about her Uncle Alistair and PAX.

She glanced around her redecorated bedroom, and not even the new Laura Ashley wallpaper with coordinating drapes and spread could make up for the fact that she wasn't in Bermuda right this minute with John.

How could Alistair have done this to her?

Last night when those three black-suited goons had deposited her in her office—which Alistair had commandeered for the duration—her fury had been magnificent.

She had raged at him for ruining her life with petty concerns like Summit conferences and global nuclear disarmament.

She had decried PAX and everyone in it, and later on, when she realized the die had already been cast, she'd cried for the first time since losing her husband.

Damn, damn, damn!

It was her own fault. She saw that now as clearly as she saw the sun shining outside her window. No one had forced her into this idiotic arrangement with the organization. Her own greed had done that for her.

When Alistair had dangled the new carpeting and expensive wallpaper and worldwide publicity in front of her eyes, she had snatched at the bait like a hungry shark.

Why was she so surprised when she got caught by the hook?

Appearances to the contrary, she wasn't a fool and, deep down, she'd known from the start that there were scores of other inns across the country that would have served PAX's purposes just as well as The White Elephant, and probably would have cost the organization less money.

The wonders that PAX had wrought were strictly Alistair's doing.

And she owed him.

Cryptography was a vital part of governmental and military communications. The airwaves were crowded; transmissions, easily tapped into. A sophisticated crypto system was necessary to secure communications between key locations.

If she did her job right, the print, voice and computer transmissions could all be encrypted in an instant and returned to plain text in the blink of an eye.

The cryptographer who usually handled sensitive situations such as Summit Meetings had been rushed to the hospital for an emergency appendectomy, leaving PAX high and dry. There simply wasn't time to pore over the records, choose a new operative and pray it all went according to plan.

Not when there was Maggie Douglass with her cursed McBride gift and sense of loyalty that were conspiring to ruin her life.

She'd tried to call John at Hideaway Haven, but PAX, in its infinite wisdom, was in the process of securing phone lines, and each time she dialed she found herself talking to her Uncle Alistair.

She'd considered bribing one of the operatives to spirit a message over to the enemy camp, but she'd probably find herself swinging from a rope if she tried it.

This PAX group was a suspicious lot.

She should know: she used to be one of them.

She thought of the ride, the pure lethal surge of desire she'd felt knowing that in a few hours they would finally be in each other's arms.

Had he gone all the way to Bermuda only to find out he'd been ditched?

Had he flung himself into the Atlantic in despair, or was he on her uncle's yacht right now with some bimbo he'd found sitting across the aisle?

Would he ever speak to her again?

Was it all over before it even started?

Did hopeless romantics forgive and forget, or did they nurse grudges of biblical proportions?

*Tune in tomorrow at the same time for the next installment of Maggie and John: Does True Love Conquer All?*

Until the Summit Meeting was over, it was anybody's guess.


SOMEWHERE OVER the Atlantic, John's anger turned to something else.

Fear.

For the past twelve hours he'd been fuming over being dumped at thirty-one thousand feet by the woman he intended to marry. His rage had been too dark for him to see the light, and when he did, it knocked the breath out of his lungs.

What if Maggie hadn't really missed the plane?

What if she'd been kidnapped?

It was a mercenary, venal world out there. You had only to pick up a magazine or turn on the radio to know just how mercenary it was. A woman with access to a seventy-foot yacht and a millionaire entrepreneur would be a choice target.

That was the good news.

The bad news was, the world was also dangerous.

Right now the woman he loved could be facing down a gunman or terrorist or—

Or she might be sunning herself on the porch of The White Elephant, sipping lemonade and flirting with another man.

Scratch that.

He'd rather fight the terrorist.

He glanced at his watch.

In two hours and fifteen minutes, he'd have his chance.


EXACTLY TWO HOURS and eighteen minutes later, John found himself up against the wall.

Literally.

He made it home in record time, jumped into his Jaguar, and zoomed up the road to The White Elephant, only to find himself stopped by a huge barbed wire fence ringing Maggie's property.

"What the hell—"

He threw the shift into park and jumped out. The vicious barbs glistened in the sun. Electric wire snaked along the top.

Anyone stupid enough to try scaling that fence would end up skewered then broiled like a shish kebab.

Sweat broke out on his forehead and behind his neck.

From behind him came a deep male voice: "This is private property, sir."

John spun around and faced two security guards big enough to be their own time zone. "I'm a friend of Ms. Douglass."

Not even a glimmer of recognition at Maggie's name. "Have you a pass to enter?"

He dug into his back pocket and pushed his wallet toward the leader. "Driver's license, American Express Platinum Card, Diner's Club."

The leader shook his head. "Sorry, sir. We don't honor these."

"The entire Western world honors these," John snapped. "I want to see Maggie."

The security guards stepped neatly in his path. "Sir, we would hate to call the police over such a small matter, but we will if you take another step toward that gate."

What the hell was going on here? These thugs talked as if they'd spent a week with Miss Manners.

John shifted both his position and his thinking.

"My apologies," he said, backing toward the Jaguar. "Next time I'll call first."

He made a U-turn and, in his rearview mirror saw them watching as he headed for the main road.

Damn right he'd call.

If he didn't see Maggie with his own eyes within the next twenty-four hours he'd call the police.

ALISTAIR WATCHED the entire episode from one of the twelve huge monitors hanging from the ceiling of Control Center.

"Should we run a check?" the taller of the two guards said into the transmitter concealed in his moustache. "We have a license plate number."

"Unnecessary," said Alistair. "He's a local innkeeper. We have a full file on him already."

*More of a file than anybody had a right to have.*

For the first time since Maggie had been returned to The White Elephant, Alistair understood what had really happened.

They were in love. Why hadn't he seen it before?

As usual, the problems of the individual had faded against the backdrop of larger, more pressing difficulties.

And, as usual, it was the individual who got hurt in the process.

He lit a cigarette and inhaled deeply.

"I made my choice a long time ago, Alistair," she'd raged at him, "and I don't regret it. Perhaps you should have done the same." She'd believed her chance for happiness with Mr. Tyler had been destroyed the moment she was spirited out of the airport.

But Maggie was wrong. It wasn't over between her and Mr. Tyler—not by any means.

Oh, PAX had thrown a metaphorical roadblock into their relationship, but what was true love without an obstacle along the way?

But as the Yankees were so fond of saying, "A man's got to do what a man's got to do."

Once the Summit Meeting was over and the dignitaries had departed in a blaze of diplomatic glory, Alistair had two very important items on his agenda: He would see to it that Maggie and John were reunited and sent packing to Bermuda and *La Jolie*; and then he would make Holland his wife.

He had the strange feeling global nuclear disarmament would probably be easier.

"JUST BRING ME a pot of coffee—no wimpy decaf stuff—and a banker's light," Maggie said to the aide Alistair had provided for her.

"I have a crypto background," the young man said, shifting nervously from one foot to the other. "I'd be glad to stick around and—"

"No, thank you," Maggie snapped. She looked up and tried to soften her words with a smile. "I work best alone."

She was drowning in information and well-meaning help. All she needed was twelve hours of uninterrupted work and, with a little luck, the system would be back up just in time for the president's arrival.

If she remembered right, output relays were a frequent trouble spot, and she'd quickly brought the system down and swapped the old output relay for a new one.

A simple solution, but in the past, simple solutions had always proved best. Maggie had always been better at cracking codes than maintaining equipment.

The crypto codes changed daily, and each morning Maggie drove to the center of the town with a huge high-tech tape recorder on the seat next to her and taped five minutes of random street-corner noise.

That street-corner noise—impossible to predict or duplicate—would be translated into a series of frequencies that would provide the key to the crypto code being used that day.

Who would have thought the sound of The Mountain Greenery's delivery truck and the blare of Alice Niedermeyer's horn would figure in world affairs?

It had been years since she'd seen any of this equipment, and those years had brought changes and modifications that made her feel as if she were swimming against the tide.

Only the McBride gift kept her from being swept out to sea.

Alistair was going out of his way to be solicitous of her feelings, but she found it difficult to manage more than a civil response to his questions.

Whenever she saw him she thought of John, and she wanted to haul off and give her uncle a good right hook. But, even though that right hook would be immensely satisfying, it wouldn't change a thing.

She was here in this arid room, surrounded by more high-tech equipment than even the Pentagon had at its disposal.

John was in Bermuda doing who-knew-what with she-didn't-want-to-know-whom.

Being a hopeless romantic was one thing; being played for a fool was something else. And the John Tyler she'd read about in *Time* and *Newsweek* and *Forbes* wasn't a man who would take kindly to being played for a fool.

The figures on the screen in front of her swam before her eyes.

The aide came back in and put a tray on the end of her desk.

"Where should I put the lamp?" he asked. "If you need it for paperwork, maybe you should—"

She covered her face with her hands, but the tears seeped through her fingers. "Just leave it," she managed. "I'll take care of it."

"No problem," he said, relentlessly helpful. "Just point me to where you want it."

She pointed to the door.

"There's no outlet over there, but I could run an extension and—" Maggie looked up at him, and he stopped. "You want me to leave?"

"Good thinking," she said, grabbing for a Kleenex.

"You're crying." Obviously an unknown concept to someone in the organization.

"I have hay fever."

He looked at her curiously and then brightened. "It's the season for it," he observed. Certainly no professional would let something as unruly as emotion get in the way of the job at hand. "I'll bring you a Contac."

The young man hurried out of the office, and as Maggie got up to lock the door behind him she didn't know whether to laugh or cry.

What she did was get back to work.

"WHAT ARE YOU DOING, Boss?" Shawna, John's assistant, tried to block his access to the master file cabinet, but he was too quick for her. "You've already destroyed half of my filing system. Are you aiming for a clean sweep?"

"I don't have time to talk about it," he said, yanking out the top drawer and dumping the contents at his feet.

"Do you mind telling me what on earth you're looking for?"

"Blueprints."

"Blueprints are kept in the safety deposit vault."

"Not these."

"Do you mind being more specific? Maybe I can help."

He crouched down, sifting through the papers piled around his ankles. "Do you remember the investigation we did into The White Elephant when we were thinking of buying up the property?"

"Vaguely," said Shawna. "Once you found out she wasn't interested, you tabled the idea."

"Well, I'm untabling it," he said, yanking out drawer number two. "I need those blueprints."

"Why didn't you say so?" Shawna stepped lightly over the papers, opened the top drawer of the map chest and extracted a thick flat envelope. "Voilà! Your blueprints."

"You're brilliant, Shawna," he said, kissing her cheek. "Remind me to raise your salary."

Shawna laughed and patted his arm. "The paperwork will be on your desk tonight," she said as she headed for the door. "Feel free to add on a Porsche while you're at it."

John nodded absently and ripped open the envelope. At that point he'd add on a Porsche, a Bentley and a private jet if the information he needed was here in the blueprints.

His terror had grown in the three hours since his encounter with the barbed wire fence and the two goons guarding it. He'd dialed all four business numbers for The White Elephant and Maggie's two private ones, only to come up each time with the recorded message: "This number is temporarily out of service."

What the hell was going on? Vivid, horrifying images of Maggie being locked in a room somewhere, unable to escape, seared his brain. She was a tough woman, Maggie Douglass was, tough and resourceful. He knew in his gut that if there was any way for her to contact him, she would have.

And that left only one explanation: she was in big trouble.

But not for long.

He spread the blueprint on top of his desk and zeroed in on the answer to his prayers.

There, just as he remembered it, was the underground passageway that would lead him straight to the woman he loved.

# Chapter Eighteen

"Don't tell me," said Holland as she saw the suitcase in Joanna's hallway, "let me guess. You've been suddenly invited on a madcap romantic weekend with your husband." She stormed into the living room, headed straight for the bar and poured herself a tumbler of Scotch. "Say hello to Alistair for me, will you?"

Joanna, her face white with shock, raced into the room after her. "I'm just going to Florida for the weekend to visit Rosie and Bert," she said. "I don't understand why you're so upset."

"Joanna, Joanna. What am I going to do with you?" She draped herself elegantly on the arm of the couch by the window. "I know you're all going someplace together. I must say you three haven't been as clever as you'd like to believe."

"Holland, is this your first drink of the day?"

Holland nodded and took a lingering sip. "Yes, my dear, it is, but I daresay it won't be my last."

Joanna sat down on the chair opposite her. "I think you've gone mad."

"You're probably right. Mad with curiosity." She polished off the rest of the Scotch. "What is it, Jo? Are you drug runners? Are you Russian spies? Do you sell secrets to alien visitors in UFO's? For two years I've been trying to figure it out.''

"Then for two years you've been wasting your time. Hasn't Alistair explained it to you before?"

"Naturally," said Holland, "but I'd love for you to explain it to me again."

"They're financiers."

Holland barely stifled a snort.

"They work the international money markets. Alistair deals with men. Ryder deals with machines."

"Where do you fit in?"

Joanna's eyes widened. "I'm married to Ryder and fond of Alistair. I work magic with makeup, Holland, not money."

"It's a good story," Holland said, wondering if she dared face Joanna's wrath and pour herself another Scotch. "It's just that I don't believe it." She leaned forward and pinned her friend with her gaze. "Why is it you always disappear whenever the two of them go off on one of their jaunts?"

Joanna didn't flinch. "I don't always disappear."

"I'm afraid you do."

"Okay, so I went with them to Gstaad last month. Who wouldn't if she had the chance?"

Holland listed fifteen cities Joanna had had the chance to visit in the last year.

"I traveled that much?" Joanna asked, seemingly shocked.

"Those are just the ones I remember," Holland said. "And when you don't go with Ryder outright, you disappear on your own."

"Suspicion doesn't become you, Holland." Joanna tugged the drapes closed, blocking out the view of the city street below. "Besides, I thought you and Alistair were finished. Why all the interest now?"

Of course Holland had no answer for that. The endless stream of flowers still continued, and so did her longing for the man responsible.

"Come with me," Joanna said suddenly. "You have this weekend off. Come with me and visit Bert and Rosie."

"You're really going to Florida?"

"I said so, didn't I?"

"And you're inviting me to come with you?"

Joanna made a show of looking around the room. "I think that was me."

"All right!" Holland stood up and reached for her purse. "This time I'm calling your bluff. I'll go to Florida with you."

That is, if the whole trip wasn't mysteriously cancelled before they even reached the airport.

Four hours later a very disappointed Holland Masters deplaned in Fort Lauderdale and kissed a very surprised Rosie Callahan hello.

"Satisfied?" Joanna whispered as they climbed into the back of Bert's Oldsmobile.

"For the moment."

They were a clever lot, she'd grant them that, but one way or another, Holland was going to get to the bottom of this or know the reason why.

"I'm TAKING A BREAK." Maggie switched off the computer and scooped up a thick stack of printouts. Her head pounded, her eyes burned, and she was famished. "I've asked that dinner be sent to my room."

Alistair, who had been working with her on the problem, looked up. "I had hoped we would dine together, Magdalena."

"No, thank you." She was scrupulously polite. "I'm going to take a nap." Never let it be said she was anything but a lady about this.

"You realize the cut happens tonight, don't you?" That was his way of asking if the problem she'd been working on nonstop would be remedied in time.

"Of course I do. That's why we've been working around the clock, isn't it?" World leaders had been arriving since midmorning, and so far they had successfully eluded the press. Rumor had it that the real work on disarmament had been done over the past six months in private negotiations, and that this Summit Meeting was to be the final, face-to-face hammering out of details.

It was an honor to be part of it, but Maggie still would rather have been in Bermuda with John.

"I appreciate all you've done," Alistair said.

She said nothing.

"Maggie." He reached and touched her forearm. She arched an eyebrow, and he quickly dropped his hand. "It will all work out," he said, and she knew it wasn't the crypto equipment he was speaking about. "Trust me on this, please."

"Trust you?" she said, heading for the door. "I'm afraid not, Alistair."

The look of sadness on his face lingered with her as she climbed the stairs to her apartment in the tower, past the swarming technicians and operatives and diplomatic attachés all scurrying to command the best position for the weekend. Her heart was hardened against her uncle, and she refused to let any other emotion dilute her righteous anger.

Not even his invitation to join the dignitaries at dinner tomorrow night was enough to soften her hard feelings.

She owed him her skills, but she didn't owe him her future, and her future was exactly what he had ruined when he had kidnapped her at the airport.

Besides, how could she ever explain this to John?

Sunday morning when the news of the Summit hit the papers, he'd know she'd been involved in something of monumental proportions. There would be questions—a lot of questions—most of which she'd be unable to answer.

Her past association with PAX was classified information. Rick hadn't known of it. Nor did Rachel or anyone else Maggie was close to.

But John wasn't Rick. He saw around the corners of her mind. He would know there was more to the choice of The White Elephant as Summit site than a fortuitous arrangement of adjoining cabins.

Of course, that was assuming John ever spoke to her again which, at the moment, seemed highly unlikely.

Dinner was waiting for her in her living room and she locked her door. The act struck her as particularly ludicrous since there wasn't a lock on God's earth that could keep a PAX operative out.

Quickly she stripped off her jeans and sweater, donned her favorite well-worn nightgown and sat down to dinner.

No matter how she was feeling about PAX and its people, she had to admit they knew how to cook.

The meals since they'd swooped down on The White Elephant had been superb.

Maybe if she'd been able to provide meals like this for paying customers she wouldn't have been tempted by PAX's offer.

The Consommé Madrilène was wonderful. The Caesar salad, incomparable. She lifted the silver lid and stared at the entrée.

Chicken Kiev.

So much for dinner.

She slammed the lid back down and, still hungry, she crawled into bed and pulled the covers over her head.

HOLLAND WINCED as she slid her jacket on over her silk dress.

The Florida sun was vicious. Her back felt raw and blistered, and she thanked God she'd slathered sun block on her face and arms before she'd joined Joanna and the two newlyweds out by the pool that afternoon.

Her director on *Destiny* was going to be surprised enough when he saw the extra four pounds she'd added. A sunburned face complete with freckles wouldn't do much to help her TV-vixen image.

She leaned forward to put the finishing touches on her eye makeup when she heard a knock on the guest room door.

"You decent, honey?"

"What passes for decent these days, Rosie?" she asked, opening the door. "Sorry if I kept you waiting. I'll just grab my bag and—"

Rosie laughed. "We're not in any rush, honey. I just came to tell you there's something in the living room you should see."

Holland looped her bag over her shoulder and followed Rosie into the hall. "Don't tell me Joanna is working on another new makeup technique," she said with a groan. "Having breakfast this morning with E.T. was enough for one weekend."

"It's not Joanna," Rosie said, practically dragging Holland toward the living room. "Just you wait until you see this."

How did Rosie manage to still sound so enthusiastic about life? Holland was half her age, and she felt old and tired.

She glanced around the room.

Joanna, looking perfectly normal, was crouched down near the television, watching another of those boring news programs that she'd been addicted to all weekend. What on earth was wrong with that woman? It seemed as if she'd switched from *Entertainment Tonight* to *The MacNeil-Lehrer Report* without a backward glance.

Nothing unusual there.

She turned and looked toward the foyer, and that's when she saw it.

Bert, a huge smile wreathing his cherubic face, was standing in the middle of more baskets of long-stemmed American Beauties than you'd find in the Rose Parade.

Her heart twisted dangerously.

"For you, honey!" Rosie pulled her over to the huge baskets. "Pretty nifty, isn't it? There's a dozen in every basket."

"A baker's dozen," Holland said, fingering the familiar ivory card.

Holland caught Joanna's eye across the room, but her friend just smiled absently and turned her attention back to her beloved news report.

"These are from that English fellow, aren't they?" Rosie prodded. "The one with the nifty Rolls-Royce?"

"Yes," Holland said. "But we're finished, Rosie. *Kaput. Finito. Sayonara.*"

Rosie hooted with laughter. ''The gent is sending you roses, and you don't want to see him? Honey, I'm eighty-two years old, and I'm here to tell you playing hard to get never works.''

Holland glared over at Joanna who was oblivious of what was going on. ''I don't know what our friend has been feeding you, Rosie, but I'm not playing hard to get. Alistair has his life and I have mine and, unfortunately that's the way it's destined to stay.''

''I hear what you're saying, Holland, but I just don't buy it,'' said Rosie sagely. ''You left him a forwarding address, didn't you?''

''No, of course not,'' Holland snapped, tossing the ivory card into her bag. ''Why would I leave him a for-warding—'' Her words died in her throat.

Her decision to come to Florida with Joanna had been so spur-of-the-moment she hadn't even had time to pack.

Not even her agent knew where to find her.

She plucked one of the bloodred roses and touched it to her cheek.

Alistair Chambers, however, was another story.

SOMETHING SMALL AND NOISY whizzed past John's face, and he hoped like hell it wasn't a bat.

For thirty minutes now he'd been picking his way through the crumbling passageway that went from be-neath the old barn cum antique shop at the edge of his property to the hidden staircase behind the west wall of the The White Elephant.

His pant legs were soaked from unexpected stumbles into holes he prayed were filled with plain water.

His nostrils burned from the heavy odor of mud and slime clinging to the walls.

The gun strapped to his chest was cold against his shirt, and he wasn't entirely sure he remembered how to use it.

He must be crazy.

He was a millionaire, wasn't he?

Donald Trump wouldn't be found crawling through an underground maze.

*Yeah, but Donald Trump isn't from Brooklyn.*

You could take the boy out of Flatbush, but you couldn't take Flatbush out of the boy.

When it came to love and business, John was strictly do-it-yourself.

MAGGIE WAS in the middle of a wonderful dream about Bermuda and John when she heard a noise.

Couldn't they leave her alone during dinner break?

She turned on her side and buried her face deeper into her pillow. If they had any decency at all, the locked door would at least make them think twice.

"Maggie."

"Go away," she mumbled. "I'm sleeping."

"Maggie, it's John."

She smiled. So she was still asleep, after all. Maybe that wonderful dream about the yacht and the sunset and the champagne would continue.

"Maggie, wake up." A hand brushed against her cheek.

Her eyes popped open. A man dressed in black stood over her. A gun was strapped to his chest. She would have screamed except he put his hand over her mouth.

"It's me."

She bit his thumb and he yelped.

"Damn it, Maggie. It's John."

She switched on her bed lamp. "Oh, my God!" She scrambled out from under the covers and threw her arms around him. "How on earth— My door was locked."

He waved a piece of silvery plastic at her. "American Express—don't leave home without it."

"The security...the fence..."

"Remember that underground passageway?"

She nodded.

"It does connect to my barn, just like I said." Apparently the passageway came up through a false wall in a third-floor bathroom. How he'd managed to elude security and find her bedroom was a mystery she didn't have time to explore.

He scooped her up from the bed. If it wasn't for the gun digging into her side, it would have been quite romantic.

"We're getting out of here."

He looked so determined that she started to laugh. "John, you're being awfully impulsive, aren't you?"

"We don't have time to lose. If they find out about this, we're finished."

"'They'? Who is 'they'?" He couldn't possibly have found out about PAX, could he?

"The people who kidnapped you. Let's get the hell out of here before they block up that passageway."

"I think you're jumping to the wrong conclusion, John. I wasn't exactly kidnapped."

"Then why weren't you on that plane to Bermuda?"

"I was detained."

"You were kidnapped."

"John, I—"

"We can quibble once we're out of here. Where's your robe?"

She pointed toward the closet. "Will you put me down? This is ridiculous."

He dropped her into an armchair near the window. "This is a hell of a way to thank someone for saving your life, Maggie."

"You're not saving my life."

"The hell I'm not."

"Go home, John. Everything is under control."

He looked like a wild man standing there with his cat-burglar clothes and that lethal weapon strapped to his body.

"I'm not going anywhere."

"Find your secret passageway and go back where you came from. I'll see you on Sunday."

"I'm not going anywhere until I find out what in hell is going on."

She found her robe and slipped it on. "Please, John, trust me on this." Alistair's very words to her not three hours ago. "There are things I can't talk about yet."

"You disappear at the airport, your phone lines are down, there's a barbed wire fence ringing your property. This place is crawling with security types—damn it, Maggie! What in hell is going on around here?" He grabbed her arm. "Come on! I'm getting you out of here now!"

She tried to pull away from him, but his strength was far superior.

"You're making this difficult, John. My uncle is here. I promise you I'm in no danger. If you could only trust me and go back home until Sunday—"

"I don't know what in hell to believe, Maggie."

"Believe me," she said, meeting his eyes. "Please, John! Just a little longer."

He pulled her up against him.

He started to say something, but his words died.

She started to protest, but couldn't remember why.

Their bodies fit together as if part of a magical plan. Nothing else mattered but that coming together.

Her blood pounded wildly through her veins, and for the first time in her life she understood why wars had been fought for love.

He moved against her, and her eyes met his.

"Maggie?" Part question, part demand.

"Yes," she said as his hands cupped her buttocks to pull her closer. "Yes, yes, yes."

The thin nightgown was no protection from the heat of his body as they tumbled to the bed, still locked in an embrace. He moved away from her for a moment and unstrapped the gun, tossing it to the floor.

She thought of the swarms of PAX operatives who might have shot first and asked questions when it was too late. "You're insane. You could have been killed!"

His mouth claimed her breasts through the silky fabric of her gown. "It didn't matter." His breath was hot and moist as he traced the outline of her nipple with his tongue. "All I could think of was finding you."

She couldn't remember ever feeling more loved.

Of course, none of this was the way she'd imagined it would be. Where was the yacht and the champagne, the soft music and the sea breezes? She'd wanted to wear silk for him, rub perfume into her pulse points for him, burn candles and light the sky for him.

In Bermuda she could have orchestrated the mood, controlled each detail, ensured perfection.

But here, in her everyday nightgown, in her everyday bed with only the sound of their hearts beating as music, she was powerless before the force of desire.

His mouth was alive against hers, his tongue hot and silky as she drew it more deeply into her mouth, running her own tongue along the silky underside until he groaned low in his throat.

He caught the hem of her nightgown between his thumb and forefinger, and the sound of the fabric splitting as he devoured her body with his eyes was something she would never forget.

Slowly he insinuated himself down her body, kissing the underside of her breasts, the inward curve of her belly, laying his face against the mound of golden curls at the top of her thighs. The rhythmic in-out of his breath drove her higher, faster, as her need grew more intense.

"John . . ." Her voice was faraway, husky and foreign to her ears. "I've never—"

"Shh," he said, making her ripple inside with pleasure as his mouth moved lower still. "Let me love you, Maggie. Let me show you."

She had only herself to offer, and to her wonderment that seemed to be quite enough.

# Chapter Nineteen

Maggie had been deeply asleep, her body curved spoon-fashion against his, when some instinct born of years of practice jolted her awake before the alarm had a chance to go off.

The room was dark, a deep velvet cave cradling them in its folds. She felt as if she'd lived a lifetime in just a few hours, as if a part of her had been but half-alive until she found John.

John slept on his right side, with the pillow bunched under his head and his left foot outside the covers.

Asleep, he didn't look like a millionaire or a motorcycle maniac or the man who owned the craziest honeymoon hotel in the Poconos.

He simply looked like the man she loved.

The sound of his breathing was sweet music. The air was heavy with the scent of sleep and passion, and if she had her way she'd spend the rest of her life there beside him.

But, unfortunately she had one final obligation before she would be free.

She eased out of bed, thankful this was a normal Sealy and not a heart-shaped water bed with a life of its own.

Now came the hard part.

John seemed to know his way around The White Elephant the way she once knew her way around Bloomingdale's. When he woke up and found her missing, he was going to come looking.

She couldn't chance having him pop up at Command Center with questions her uncle wouldn't care to answer.

She pulled on her clothes and tiptoed out of the bedroom. It wasn't a bad place, after all, a nice two-bedroom apartment complete with full bath and kitchen and a wonderful view of Mount Snow.

He should be very happy there until she got back.

And if he wasn't, she'd deal with that later.

With apologies to the man she loved, she double-locked the door behind her and slipped the key into her pocket.


CLICK.

*Click.*

John opened his eyes and squinted into the darkness.

The side of the bed next to him was empty, and unless he missed his bet, that was Maggie double locking him into the room.

She thought one lock wasn't enough to keep him in.

He had to admit he was kind of flattered.

But he had news for her: She could hang a half dozen Medecos on that door, and it wasn't going to make one damned bit of difference.

The passageway John had used to enter the house terminated right in her pink-tiled bathroom not ten feet away and that, in turn, connected with a series of catwalks providing access to almost every part of the house.

Somehow things had gotten away from him. The second they came together on that narrow bed of hers he forgot about kidnappers and terrorists and the dangers of modern life and found himself sinking deeper into the wonders of love.

She was right, Maggie was. Heart-shaped tubs and mirrored ceilings were fun, but when it was as right between a man and woman as it was right between Maggie and him, none of that really mattered a damn.

Since the beginning of time all that was needed was a man and a woman and a place to be alone. It was as simple as that, and until now, that hard to come by for them.

He could still taste her, like smoked honey, on his lips and tongue, feel the hard rasp of her nipples against the palms of his hands. The way she'd been so hot and tight for him, opening slowly around him then bringing him home to where he belonged, where he'd always belonged.

This was their beginning, the start of loving each other, supporting each other, growing old with each other.

But they'd never have that chance if he lost her now.

"Trust me," she'd said. "I'm in no danger."

That might be true, but he couldn't bank on it.

She'd saved his life in the Bronze Penguin.

That night in his driveway she'd been willing to fight off a trio of Hell's Angels to keep him safe.

That fierce protective instinct might still be at work, keeping him locked in this room while she faced danger alone.

Over his dead body.

He leaped up and grabbed for his clothes.

Maybe Maggie couldn't tell him what was going on, but there was no law that said he couldn't find out for himself.

SHE DID IT, but then Alistair had never doubted she could.

Maggie leaned back in her chair and surveyed the equipment purring smoothly all around her.

"For a woman who just worked ten hours straight, you're looking quite cheerful," Alistair observed.

Maggie looked up, a slight smile on her lovely face. "Amazing what a nap can do."

"I'd assumed it had something to do with the miracle you performed here with the crypto equipment. We're in your debt, my girl."

She'd never been good at accepting compliments, and she shrugged awkwardly. "I did what had to be done, that's all."

But, of course, Maggie had done much more. It was in her nature to extend herself beyond her reach and push for a higher degree of perfection.

Alistair sat on the edge of her desk. "Your Mr. Tyler tried to storm the grounds yesterday." He watched her face carefully for her reaction.

"He did?"

"The man is determined to find you, Magdalena. If this house weren't so secure, I'd almost expect to see him come walking down the hall."

Her eyes fluttered shut for a second. "Oh, I don't think that's going to happen."

"A man in love is not a rational being. He is capable of anything."

"I'll keep that in mind."

It was time to confront her.

"I know he's in this house, my girl."

She said nothing.

"We have heat sensors everywhere. You're fortunate it was I who saw the fluctuation in your apartment."

Her face flamed red and she looked down, but he could see the flicker of a smile trying to break through.

"Have you nothing to say?"

She looked up, and he saw what she'd been trying to hide since that first afternoon at the Bronze Penguin.

His Magdalena was madly in love.

"He thought I was in danger, Ally. When your bozos kidnapped me from the airport—" She was radiant with pleasure. "Well, you can imagine what he thought."

"Your knight on a white charger?"

She grinned. "He *is* impetuous, isn't he?"

"More than you realize."

Her face drained of blood. "What do you mean? Has something happened?"

"He's no longer in your apartment."

She jumped up from her chair. "That's impossible. I locked him in." She pushed her hair off her face, and he could see her hands were shaking. "I double locked him in."

"The fact remains, your apartment is empty."

"Oh, my God," she moaned. "Ally, he's carrying a gun. The treaty is due to be signed in less than an hour. If any of the security people find him, they'll—"

He put an arm on her shoulder to steady her although his own adrenaline was pumping hard and fast.

"Come with me."

He hurried her through the winding halls filled with security agents from the four major powers. They stopped at a door labeled *O* that was guarded by a huge man who hadn't smiled since the Magna Carta. After flashing their badges and going through a metal detector, the door was unlocked, and Alistair ushered Maggie inside.

"This is the heat-sensing unit," he said, beginning to run a check. "It's our best means to locate him. Do you have any idea how he got into The White Elephant in the first place?''

''A secret passageway,'' she said, leaning over his shoulder. ''He has a copy of the original blueprints.''

''Where is the passageway?''

''I don't know exactly. I didn't get to—I mean we never . . .'' Her voice trailed away into uncomfortable silence.

Alistair bit back a smile. There would be time later for that, God willing.

A high-pitched tone filled the air.

''There!'' Alistair said, leaning forward to point out a small blip on the screen. ''Angling down between the second and third floor.''

''If he keeps going in that direction,'' Maggie said, ''he'll end up near the Treaty Room.''

Alistair unlocked his leather pouch and brought out a flat identification card. Then he quickly ran it through a thermal printer.

''You're going to have to go in and find him, Maggie, and when you do, dispose of the firearm and make certain he keeps this pass on him at all times.''

''What if I don't find him in time? Can you—''

''You'll find him.''

''He's a smart man. How do I explain this to him? What do I say?''

''Whatever needs to be said.'' In a few hours the Summit Meeting would be a matter of public record, and he wasn't going to sacrifice her future the way he might have sacrificed his own.

She hesitated a moment, then bent down and kissed his cheek.

The last of the barriers between them disappeared, and Alistair rejoiced.

"Thanks, Ally," she whispered, and in a flash she was gone.

THE BLUEPRINTS WERE WRONG.

John had been travelling in the general direction laid out in the plans, but unfortunately those plans were the originals and didn't take additions into account.

By his calculations he should have been over the room he knew to be Maggie's office where there was a trick door behind the bookshelves.

He pushed at the wall, trying to ignore the slick wetness beneath his hands. Nothing. Not even the slightest indication that this wall was anything but solid.

They really knew how to make them back in 1799, didn't they?

He'd been back there for hours. His head pounded from trying to peer into the darkness, and his muscles were cramping from the half crouch he was in, thanks to those damned low ceilings.

A while back he'd heard voices, and he'd stretched himself out flat on the ground, ear pressed to the slightest crack where light filtered up at him. He couldn't understand anything the two men were saying, but he knew the word *Nyet* when he heard it.

Either The White Elephant had gone international, or Maggie had somehow gotten herself involved in something more dangerous than he'd ever dreamed.

She'd said her uncle was on the premises. She'd never been clear on what the man actually did for a living, but if that Rolls-Royce and those fancy suits of his were any indication, whatever Alistair Chambers did he was handsomely rewarded for it.

*She could be part of it, too,* a small voice reminded him.

The White Elephant's financial troubles were well documented. He had the facts and figures stacked neatly in a file beside his desk. She could have fallen into a trap lined with dollar bills.

"Damn it to hell!" He cracked into a wall where no wall was supposed to be.

This sneaking around inside the walls was getting him no place. If he could only get back to her apartment he could put his suspicions to her, and maybe she would explain what in hell was going on.

He was beginning to have visions of himself as a dusty bag of bones with only his Rolex watch and his dental work to identify him by.

He tried to orient himself. There! About fifty yards up ahead. A small shaft of light was filtering sideways. He moved toward it, picking his way over crumbled rock and splintered boards. Maybe that was one of the secret doors he'd been looking for. Maybe over the years it had warped, and he'd be able to pry it open.

Maybe—

"Drop the gun, John!"

He turned and looked at Maggie Douglass.

Maybe it was all over.


HE LOOKED SO DANGEROUS standing there in the darkness with that gun in his hand that it took Maggie a moment to recover her equilibrium.

"Listen to me, John! If they find you with a gun, they'll shoot you first and ask questions later."

"Damn it, Maggie! First you skip out of the airport and I end up in Bermuda alone, and now you lock me in your bedroom and disappear for half a day. What the hell's going on around here?"

She handed him the ID badge Alistair had made up. "Put this on," she ordered, hoping she sounded more authoritative than she felt, "and leave the damned gun on the ground. You're in enough danger right now as it is."

"Danger?" He peered at the ID badge. "What kind of danger?"

"Not the kind you think."

"I read *Spycatcher*," he said, lowering the gun to his side. "I know what goes on."

Her laughter bounced off the walls of the passageway. "And I suppose you think James Bond movies tell it like it is."

"Nice work if you can get it."

"Well, now you've got it, John." She gestured toward their surroundings. "Pretty glamorous, isn't it?"

"What the hell are you trying to say, Maggie?"

"First drop the gun. It's bad enough you're crawling around inside the walls. If Russian security finds you with a gun—" she mimed a shiver "—Siberia."

He bent down and placed the gun on the ground.

"I'm an American citizen." She could hear the beginning of a laugh in his voice. "They can't send me to Siberia."

She snapped her fingers. "An exchange program. It happens all the time."

From the other side of the wall she heard the sound of voices and footsteps as the Treaty Room filled with people.

"It's too late," she whispered, motioning for John to be quiet. "We have to stay put until it's over."

"Maggie—" She clamped her hand over his mouth.

"Come with me, John," she whispered, leading him up the catwalk. "There's something I think you should see."

IT WASN'T EVERY DAY you crouched on a catwalk thirty feet in the air, peered through a concealed peephole and watched the four most powerful leaders on earth sign a treaty pledging to make this a safer, saner world.

He glanced at Maggie crouching next to him, her coppery-blond hair falling across her face.

It wasn't every day you found out the woman you love could give 007 a run for his money.

The leaders rose from the table and embraced one another as the room erupted into applause. He still didn't know what the hell they were signing, but from the smile on the president's face it was something pretty damned good.

"You *are* on our side," he whispered, still transfixed by the scene below.

"Of course I am," she said, leaning over and kissing the side of his mouth. "What a silly question."

It was a good thing they were still applauding below because his laughter broke through. "If you think that question is silly, wait until you hear the rest of them, Maggie."

"No secrets, John," she said, her voice soft and true. "I promise."

He took her hand and together they watched history in the making.

# Chapter Twenty

It was raining when Holland's plane landed at JFK, a dark, hot, miserable rain that suited her just fine.

In her present mood, Florida's constant sunshine, coupled with Rosie and Bert's connubial bliss, was too out of sync with reality.

All the way home she'd badgered Joanna mercilessly, but her friend stuck to her story: not even Ryder had known Holland made the trip to Florida.

If Joanna knew how Alistair had discovered that fact, she wasn't saying. Besides, she was so engrossed in this sudden passion for news that Holland had finally left her to her copies of *The New York Times* and *The Philadelphia Inquirer*.

For a change, luck was with her. She found a cab to take her back to Manhattan, and within an hour she was curled up with a cup of coffee and the next day's script.

Her phone messages had amounted to nothing—naturally no call from Alistair. But there had been three calls from the florist informing her that a dozen red roses were awaiting delivery.

He even knew when she was coming home. If she wasn't so tired, she'd search her apartment for a hidden camera.

The TV was on low, and she was taping an interview with Gloria Steinem, who was explaining how to live a great life without a man. That from a woman who'd probably never been without a man in her life.

Suddenly a male voice broke through. "We interrupt this program to bring you a special report."

Probably another politician caught with his finger in the shredder. So what else was new?

"We're standing here at the foot of Mount Snow in East Point, Pennsylvania."

East Point? Wasn't that right around where Maggie Douglass had her inn?

"History is being made here this afternoon."

Either she was going crazy, which was a distinct possibility, or that was The White Elephant looming behind Peter Jennings.

"A major step was taken today toward total nuclear disarmament. In a small country inn tucked away in the Pocono Mountains, the leaders from the four superpowers met in secret and—"

Holland reached for her eyeglasses and popped them on.

That certainly *did* look like The White Elephant, but then there must be dozens of quaint country inns in the Poconos.

"...the press secretary said the formal signing of the document is going on at this moment, to be followed by a press conference wherein..."

Wait a minute!

There in the back, right behind a huge barbed wire fence was a man who looked remarkably like Alistair.

Maybe she'd had too much sun this weekend. Alistair Chambers at a Summit Meeting held at his niece's inn?

Ridiculous.

"Complete details on this surprise Summit on the evening news."

She quickly rewound the tape and pressed the play button.

There was Peter Jennings. There was the barbed wire fence. She got down on her knees directly in front of the screen.

"My God!" She rocked back on her heels, hands shaking. It *was* Alistair, wearing the navy-and-gray silk tie she'd bought for him at Bijan three weeks ago.

She backed the tape up a few inches and froze it again. As if Alistair weren't a big enough surprise, there was Ryder O'Neal lurking behind him. That shock of wild hair was a dead giveaway.

Holland didn't know whether to laugh or cry, so she did both.

He wasn't a gunrunner or a smuggler or a financier with a string of fast horses and faster women.

He wasn't married or gay or crazy.

She still didn't know exactly what he *was* but she knew what he wasn't, and at the moment that was enough.

She'd forgive him a weekend with Maggie Thatcher any day.

And she intended to tell him so in person.

THE SUMMIT MEETING was over.

Beyond the window of his temporary office at The White Elephant, the last of the shiny black limousines disappeared en route to the airport, and Alistair breathed easy for the first time in months.

The disarmament treaty had far exceeded expectation, and a sense of cautious euphoria had everyone smiling.

He glanced over at Maggie and John who had been sitting by the window for hours now, watching presidents and prime ministers, and holding hands.

The sight of that simple connection between them made him think of Holland.

His resignation had been drafted, and as soon as Air Force 1 was airborne he would submit it for approval.

But he suspected Holland's approval would be harder to come by.

Straightening his tie, he walked toward his niece and extended his hand. "You did a fine job, Magdalena," he said as she stood up to embrace him. "I am prouder of you than I know how to say." His voice cracked unexpectedly, and for the first time in many years he made no attempt to disguise his emotion. "You are more like Sarah than I ever realized."

Maggie's eyes glistened with tears, and she kissed his cheek. "Thank you," she said softly. "I'll treasure that."

Tyler sat quietly on the couch, watching them, his eyes intelligent and thoughtful.

He was a good man, this John Adams Tyler, the kind of man Alistair had always wished his beloved niece would find. His intelligence and sensitivity were balanced by an impetuous, romantic nature that should make the years ahead interesting to watch unfold.

Alistair started to say something to him when he heard his name.

"Chambers?" One of his aides popped up at the door. "We have a problem."

Maggie and John fell silent.

"Serious?"

The young man shrugged. "You'd better come with me."

He followed the young man out of the room with Maggie and John close behind him.

"Is it a problem with the motorcade?" he asked. "Difficulties at the airport?"

The young man said nothing. Alistair followed him through the main lobby and outside.

"Over there by the gate," said the aide, a huge smile breaking across his serious face. "Someone wants to speak with you."

Alistair turned. The fence was being dismantled. Stacks of wood and wire were piled along the perimeter, and the only section still standing was the gate.

And that's where she was.

Framed in the opening stood Holland Masters, surrounded by baskets of long-stemmed red roses.

Eyes brimming, he made his way toward her.

"A baker's dozen?" he asked, stopping just inches away from her.

She met his eyes. "A baker's dozen."

"We have a great deal to discuss, Holland."

She whispered something low, for his ears alone, and he pulled her into his arms and opened his heart.

"Yankee ingenuity," he said softly. "Why didn't I think of that?"

MAGGIE SIGHED as she watched her uncle and Holland head toward the Rolls-Royce. "I love happy endings."

John looked down at her. "How do you know there's going to be a happy ending? Holland still doesn't know what he does for a living. How will he explain it the next time he disappears like that?"

Maggie snapped her fingers. "Easy as pie," she said. "He's quitting the organization."

"I'll be damned," John muttered. "Just when I thought I'd be in for high adventure."

"Oh, you'll be in for plenty of high adventure, Mr. Tyler," she said with a laugh. "From here on in, The White Elephant is going to give you a real run for your money." The Summit Meeting had ended less than five hours ago, and already reservations were lighting up her switchboard.

He grinned and tugged at a lock of her hair. "Give it your best shot, Maggie. I love a good fight."

Maggie swayed on her feet as a wave of bone-crushing fatigue swept over her.

"Are you okay?" he asked, putting his arm around her for support.

"Exhausted," she said, leaning against him. How solid he was. How strong and good and true. "It's been quite a day."

He swept her up into his arms. "I'll take you back inside. You need some sleep."

He pressed a kiss to her mouth, and suddenly she wasn't quite so tired any longer.

"They're dismantling everything inside," she said, tilting her head toward The White Elephant. "It's so loud, so—"

His eyebrows arched. "Don't tell me you want to go back to my place?"

"Don't sound so surprised, Johnny," she said with a soft laugh. "If I'm going to fight you for Pocono supremacy, shouldn't I take another look at what I'm up against?"

"Think carefully, Maggie—mirrored ceilings, sunken tubs, roaring fireplaces. You might find yourself compromised."

She kissed him at the corner of his mouth. "That's what I'm counting on. Now that we're involved—"

"We're not involved," he interrupted as they headed toward her car.

Her heart lurched. "We're not?"

He leaned against the Jeep, with Maggie still in his arms. "We're getting married."

Her breath caught. "Married?"

"Married."

"Speak for yourself, John." A wonderful flutter built deep inside. "You Brooklyn boys are so domineering."

He pulled her closer. "Say you love me."

"I love you, John Adams Tyler. I think I always have."

They went back to Hideaway Haven to make some history of their own.

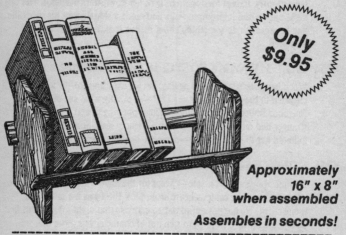

# *Harlequin American Romance*

## COMING NEXT MONTH

### #253 TAKING A CHANCE by Robin Francis

Paulette D'Amboise was in danger of becoming the Holly Golightly of Madison, Wisconsin. Men fought to take her out; no one thought to take her seriously. Except for Jonathan Day, her downstairs neighbor. Her all-night parties and impromptu visits had made a shambles of his sober life, and he meant to do something about it. But Jonathan did so at his own peril....

### #254 CALL MY NAME SOFTLY by Ginger Chambers

When her hometown turned against her for exposing corruption, Anne retreated to the beach for peace. That was exactly what she didn't find. Neighbor Robert and his young son kept popping in and a mysterious stranger had more on his mind than a friendly visit. Someone had followed her to her hideaway—someone bent on murderous revenge.

### #255 GOING BACK by Judith Arnold

Daphne always played it safe—except for the night when as a lovelorn co-ed she seduced the campus heartthrob. Now Brad was her latest real estate client. He had a surefire way to exorcise that night forever, but first he had to convince Daphne to step out of character one more time....

### #256 COME HOME TO ME by Marisa Carroll

Laurel Sauder was in town for a few weeks filling in at her father's pharmacy. Special Agent Seth Norris was passing through accompanying the President on a whistle-stop tour. Laurel and Seth would have one night together. And out of that night would come a baby, created out of loneliness and love. But would that night be a beginning for Seth, too, a night his heart found a home?

The passionate saga that brought you SARAH and
ELIZABETH continues in the compelling,
unforgettable story of

# Catherine

# MAURA SEGER

An independent and ambitious woman earns the disapproval of Boston society when she discovers passion and
love with Irishman Evan O'Connel.

# *Harlequin American Romance*

## With Barbara Bretton, the password is adventure

Maggie and John discovered that getting involved with Uncle Alistair and PAX meant nonstop action and hijinks. But how could they complain when it also brought them each other?

Catch all the exploits of the men and women of PAX, as Ryder O'Neal, electronics wizard, and Joanna Stratton, master of disguises, join forces to save the royal family—and become one of their own—in #193 *Playing for Time.*

And don't miss the chilling climax when Max Steel's and Kelly Madison's commitment and fortitude are put to the ultimate test in #274 *A Fine Madness*, coming in December 1988.

Join Barbara Bretton's PAX organization . . . and experience the adventure!

---